DEATH ON THE RHINE

Germany 1923 The beaten Fatherland is in turmoil, inflation is raging and millions are unemployed. Adolf Hitler is raising a right-wing traditionalist Germany to march on Berlin and Von Horn, the perverted head of the secret German Intelligence Unit, plans to murder the Command-in-Chief of the British Army of the Rhine. 'C', head of MI6, orders 'Common Smith' VC to sail secretly for the army HQ at Cologne and prevent the planned assassination. 'C' warns him that if he fails, then the whole of Germany will be re-united under a fanatic, who will lead them into another terrible war against Western Europe.

DEATH ON THE RHINE

DEATH ON THE RHINE

by

Charles Whiting

Magna Large Print Books
Long Preston, North Yorkshire,
BD23 4ND, England.

British Library Cataloguing in Publication Data.

Whiting, Charles
Death on the Rhine.

A catalogue record of this book is available from the British Library

ISBN 0-7505-1817-0

First published in Great Britain 1994
by Severn House Publishers Ltd.

Published in Large Print 2002 by arrangement with
Eskdale Publishing

Magna Large Print is an imprint of Library Magna Books Ltd.

Printed and bound in Great Britain by
T.J. (International) Ltd., Cornwall, PL28 8RW

PRELUDE TO A MURDER

'The very best way to die is to pass out fighting when your blood is up and you feel nothing.'

Winston Churchill, 1945

As they sang the final hymn that Sunday in the open air, the top brass could hear the heavy guns still thundering. To the east, the horizon was ablaze with fire. Overhead a Dakota limped back to base, trailing thick black smoke from its port engine. This was Palm Sunday, but the war still continued in all its bitter fury.

Behind the Great Man, dressed for this warlike jaunt in the uniform of his old regiment, the Fourth Hussars, a staff officer whispered to a colleague, 'Old Jerry's just put in another counter-attack. But we're beating the beggars all right!' The Great Man smiled and, sucking hard on his loose false teeth, launched into the last verse of *'Onward Christian Soldiers'* with renewed vigour.

The padre blessed the assembly and then hurried away to help tend the fresh batch of wounded being ferried across the broad, flowing Rhine near the wrecked bridge.

The service finished, the Great Man lit a huge cigar and turned to the Supreme Allied Commander, standing next to him in the open German field. 'Well, my dear General,' he chortled expansively, bland, broad face wreathed in blue smoke, 'we've got him. The German is whipped.'

As if to emphasize the Great Man's words, a Spitfire came in, barrelling low, rolling over and over in a victory roll, before surging high into the grey March sky once again. Obviously, he had just shot down a German plane and wanted everyone to know it.

General Eisenhower, his face worn and pale hands shaking a little as they held one of the sixty cigarettes he smoked a day, nodded. It had been a long campaign. It was now nine months since his troops had landed in Normandy. There had been a lot of tough decisions, failures and heartaches since then. Now, at last, they had crossed Germany's last great natural barrier. Thank God, the Great Man was right. Germany was virtually whipped. The war in Europe was almost over.

For a little while the two of them and the rest of the top brass peered at the far bank of the Rhine through their binoculars. More and more troops were being ferried across into the smoke and fire of the battle being waged there. Dakotas were coming in low to drop supplies by chute to the hard-pressed paratroopers who were fighting for their lives at the van of the huge attack.

Time and time again the Great Man's face lit up when he saw something which pleased him. Once or twice he stamped his right foot like a spoiled child watching some exciting new game. Finally he lowered his glasses and lit another cigar. 'General,' he said almost playfully to Eisenhower, gesturing to one of the landing barges that had just come from the other side of the great river, 'I'd like to get into that boat and cross.'

Eisenhower's customary broad grin vanished. 'No, Mr Prime Minister,' he said firmly. 'I'm the Supreme Commander and I refuse to let you go across. You might get killed.'

The Great Man pouted like a spoiled child, but obeyed.

Half an hour later, when Eisenhower had gone to visit his troops, the Great Man sprang into action. He turned to the sharp-faced, birdlike Field Marshal in charge of the great crossing and said, 'Monty, why don't we go across and have a look at the other side?'

Surprisingly enough, Montgomery, who previously had always objected to having the Great Man on the scene when he was fighting a battle – he 'cluttered up the place too much' – said, 'Why not?'

Churchill broke out into a big smile. He shouted to the top brass, 'Now that General Eisenhower is gone, I'm going across.' He winked at them boyishly.

Minutes later they were standing on the eastern bank in brilliant sunshine. With a crump the first German shell landed yards away. Earth and gravel showered upwards. One or two of the top brass flinched or ducked instinctively. Not Churchill. Cigar jutting out of the side of his mouth, he stroke forward at a cracking pace. Hurriedly, the reluctant top brass followed.

In the end, as tracer from a machine gun began to zip lethally through the air from a ruined barn to the right, it was too much for General Simpson, commander of the US 9th Army. He said to Montgomery, 'This is no place for the PM.'

Montgomery shrugged, as if it was no concern of his.

Simpson said, 'I'd hate to have anything happen to him in my army area.' He looked at Churchill. The Great Man was striding forward, puffing out smoke furiously, as if he would never stop.

The machine gun had been joined now by a German multiple mortar. With an ear-splitting howl, six great shells were streaking up into the sky, trailing thick black smoke behind them.

Simpson acted. He caught up with the Great Man and said pointedly, 'If we keep on going, we'll soon be in the front line.'

Reluctantly, Churchill allowed himself to be returned to the river, but he wasn't finished yet. He still wanted to have fun.

He made the top brass take him to where

a great iron railway bridge, which had been partially destroyed by the retreating Germans, had fallen into the river. Again in the lead, Churchill simply clambered on to it, as if he was a man in his twenties and not in his sixties. Reluctantly, the others followed.

Now the German gunners on the other bank started to home in on the bridge. Shells howled out of the sky. Great geysers of whirling wild, white water erupted. And they were coming closer. It was almost as if the Germans knew that Adolf Hitler's most implacable enemy was on that bridge. With a great hollow boom, a shell hit the other side of the bridge. The whole structure vibrated. Shrapnel flew everywhere. A junior officer rushed to General Simpson. 'Sir ... sir!' he cried excitedly, above the racket, 'we're bracketed already. One or more tries and they'll hit us!'

Simpson had had enough. He caught up with the joyful Churchill, who was revelling in the excitement and danger, as he had always done since he had been a subaltern fighting the 'fuzzy-wuzzies', as he called them in the previous century. 'There are snipers in front of you, Prime Minister!' he yelled. 'They are shelling both sides of the bridge and now they have started to shell the road behind you. I cannot accept the responsibility for your being here and must ask you to come away now.'

A look came on the Great Man's face which reminded Montgomery of a little boy being called away from his sandcastles on the beach.

Churchill didn't react. Instead he grasped one of the bridge's girders with both arms, peering over his shoulder at Simpson as if challenging the American general to pry him loose.

Montgomery decided it was time to act. He snapped in that brisk, high-pitched voice of his, making his 'r's' sound like 'w's', 'My God, Prime Minister, the war's nearly over! You don't want the Huns to kill you at this stage of the game, do you?'

Churchill's look of petulance vanished. He stared back at the little Field Marshal calmly. 'My dear Monty,' he said slowly, 'twenty-two years ago on this same river a certain – then unknown – Austrian upstart tried to have me killed.'

Montgomery gasped audibly. He knew that Churchill had led an adventurous early life. But he knew nothing of an attempt to assassinate him on the River Rhine nearly a quarter of a century before. 'What!' he said somewhat stupidly.

The Great Man smiled. He released his grip on the girder and allowed himself to be led back to the barge. 'Yes,' he said, pleased to have startled and bewildered the generals, 'he failed then and I doubt if Herr Hitler is going to kill me now. Gentlemen, I think I could do with a large – a very large – whisky and soda…’

BOOK ONE

ORDERS TO SAIL

'He who eats with the Devil needs a long spoon.'

Old German Proverb

ONE

Almost noiselessly, the killers paddled the little rubber boat through the still water. On the Rhine nothing moved. The barges lay at anchor and the water police patrol boat had long past.

To their front, Cologne's great cathedral rose out of the night, a great ragged shadow towering over the city, now silent and shrouded in sleep. For it was two in the morning and even the city's red light district next to the main station had closed down.

There were four of them, dressed in black, with peaked caps pulled down low over their brutal, war-hardened faces. They knew what they were about to do would cause a great outcry – that's why they were intent on doing it. Thereafter, they would all be hunted men, but they had been hunted before. The chase was nothing new to them. Besides, they were prepared to give their lives for the holy cause of a re-united Fatherland.

'Dadrüben!' their leader hissed urgently. He tugged impatiently at the black patch which hid the socket of his left eye – blown

out at Verdun in 1916.

The other three started to steer the little boat in the direction he indicated. Now they could see the vague outline of the steam pinnace, tied to the quayside just below the cathedral. No lights showed, not even mooring lights. But they had expected that. As their leader had growled the previous night when orders had come from Munich to carry out the assassination, 'You know the Tommies – spend all their time drinking that weak tea of theirs? Was like that in the trenches. Too busy making tea to fight a real war. They'll be asleep all right, mark my words.'

They had nodded sagely. They were all veterans of the hard-fighting of four years in the trenches on the Western Front; they knew their Tommies all right.

Now they were almost up to the boat. It was sleek and white and on its stern hung the hated flag of the English navy, that navy which had virtually starved Imperial Germany into surrender five years before in 1918. On board slept the man who had instituted that blockade, Winston Churchill. That was why the Leader in Munich had picked him as the victim. It would be yet another signal to the German people that all was not lost; that there was still hope in their occupied, beaten country; that the New Germany was on the march at last.

'Ship your paddles,' the man with the patch hissed. Noiselessly, they did as he commanded. Under its own momentum the rubber boat continued towards the silent English craft. The man with the patch shot a sharp glance to left and right. The towpath that ran the length of the bank was empty. The Tommy sentries were either not posted or asleep. He smiled to himself. Someone would get a 'cigar' thrust into him on the morrow when the Tommies discovered how slack they had been.

'Anton,' he commanded. 'You – the stern.'

The man nodded. Expertly, he reached up, grasped the brass handrail and tugged himself on board, crouching there tensely.

'Gregor – the bows.'

A second man went up and onto the craft.

Now the man with the patch could hear someone snoring loudly from within. Again he smiled to himself. The Englishman, and he hoped the snorer was the hated Winston Churchill, wouldn't be snoring much longer. 'Theo, you come with me.' Balancing a little awkwardly in the rubber boat, he reached up and pulled himself on board. Theo followed.

Now all four of them were aboard the enemy craft. There was no sound, save that of the snorer and the soft lap-lap of the water against the boat.

The man with the patch raised his right arm and held it there for a full minute, while he counted off the seconds. It was the signal. And they all saw it. All four of them took out the bombs which had been sent with their orders from Munich, and bending, armed them. The soft tick of the time clock seemed hellish loud to the man with the patch. But nothing stirred on the boat. No one had heard. Below the snorer continued to do so noisily.

Now the four of them set about finding a hiding place for the explosive devices. They were timed to go simultaneously, in twenty minutes, which would give them time to get across the river again into Unoccupied Germany. There arrangements had been made for them to motor to Munich. From there they would cross the border into Austria and lie low till the hue-and-cry was over. As the Leader had told them before they had set out on their mission, 'The English will make a great song-and-dance. There will be diplomatic outrage and those traitors in Berlin will assist them in attempting to find the culprits. But you will not be found, my brave comrades.' And his hard Austrian face had broken momentarily into a tight smile. '*Never!* And while the English and their damned Berlin lackeys seek you out, the German people will know that *we* have struck another blow for Germany's freedom. *Heil!*'

As one, their harsh faces glowing with

pride and faith, they had sprung to their feet before him and thrust up their right arms in the new salute of their party, bellowing, 'Heil Hitler!...'

Fifty yards away, shrouded in the shadows of the great Hohenzollern Bridge which spanned the river there, Private Mick Taggart pulled the contraceptive off, tied up his flies and reached in his pocket. Leaning against the wall, Lala pulled on her knickers and adjusted her garters. She yawned. She was tired. She had just come from the *'Bal Musette'*, but it had been a slack night in the brothel and as was her custom when her takings were low, she usually serviced one or two of the Tommies who guarded the Rhine on her way back to her room. It was hard, cold work, doing it in the open, but the bored, lonely Tommy sentries were appreciative and were inclined to pay more than her normal customers these days.

'Zigaretten or *geld?'* Private Taggart asked.

'Beide – both,' she answered. She could sell the fine English cigarettes on the black market.

Taggart laughed. He slapped her silk-clad, plump bottom appreciatively and said, *'Do gut jig-jig. Hier,* ten Woodbines and a five mark note. I really enjoyed th-' He stopped short. Something was moving on the steam pinnace.

'Was ist los?' the whore asked, as he bent

low and swung his head slowly from left to right.

He didn't answer. He was using an old trick he'd learned in the trenches. It was the way to spot a dark object at night. There it was – somebody moving on the deck of the boat.

'Cor ferk a duck!' he muttered to himself, 'and with his nibs on board.'

'Was ist los?' the whore repeated her query.

By way of an answer he took her by the elbow and propelled her deeper into the shadow of the great bridge. 'Get out of the way,' he whispered urgently. *'Schnell.* There might be trouble.'

Hastily, Taggart grabbed his rifle and bayonet which he had leaned up against the stone wall while he had been occupied with the whore. Taggart was a brave man. He had won the military medal at Ypres in '15 and the three gold wound stripes on his sleeve bore testimony that he had shed his blood for his country more than once. But four years in the trenches had taught him to be cautious. 'Don't stick yer neck out,' he had always lectured reinforcements, 'cos ole Jerry's more and likely to chop it frigging well orff!' Now, he approached the boat, rifle tucked into his hip, walking on the side of his hobnailed boots so that he made as little noise as possible.

Already he had spotted two more mysterious figures on the boat and the way they moved, cautiously and half crouched, told him that they were up to no good. Recently, in Occupied Cologne, there had been a lot of talk of lonely British soldiers being waylaid and beaten up. One rumour had it that a British secretary working for the Control Commission had been raped and badly beaten up, while her officer boyfriend had been murdered and tossed in the Rhine. Taggart was an old sweat with ten years service behind him. He had long since given up paying much attention to rumours. Still, he told himself, where there's smoke, there's fire. Those mysterious figures were out to get Churchill, he was sure of it now.

He was ten yards away from the boat now. The men on the boat made hardly a sound as they moved about, but he could hear someone snoring within the craft. Carefully, he clicked off his safety catch. He already had a bullet in the breach of the Lee Enfield. 'Always keep one up the spout,' was his motto, 'cos yer never knows when yer gonna need it.'

Now he knelt down to present the smallest possible target. It was against Army regulation to challenge in that position. But Private Mick Taggart had survived so long because he had always interpreted Army regulations in his own manner. 'Who goes there?' he barked, his voice seeming to be very loud.

'Scheisse!' one of the men on the boat cursed. *'Die Tommies!'*

Crack! Scarlet flame stabbed the gloom. A bullet howled off the stonework next to Taggart, showering his face with splinters. Behind, under the bridge, the whore screamed.

'Ferk this for a tale!' Taggart yelled angrily. He pressed the trigger. On the craft one of the dark figures shrieked in sudden pain. He flung up his hands dramatically. Next moment he went over backwards and dropped into the water with a splash.

In an instant, all was chaos. As Taggart fired again, lights went on everywhere in the boat. There were angry shouts. Someone shrilled on a whistle. Down the towpath there came the sound of heavy boots running. A man dived over the side. Taggart caught him in mid-dive. He yelped with pain and fell into the rubber boat, moaning. Taggart grinned and shouted to no one in particular, 'Two frigging down and two to frigging go!' He fired once more.

Next moment a harsh official voice commanded, 'All right, cease firing out there. *Cease firing!* We've nabbed the other two.'

'Sir!' Taggart answered smartly and rose to his feet, suddenly aware that the whore was still under the bridge and a used french letter lay in the towpath. He turned, white torches flashed on the deck and whispered urgently. 'Bugger off, Frowlein. Mark schnell ... bugger orff!' There was the sound of high heels running and Taggart breathed a sigh of relief. He knew what the orderly sergeant would do to him if he found he had been with a woman while on sentry-go. As he'd heard so many commanding officers say to him in the past, as he had stood smartly to attention, flanked by two regimental police. 'Your trouble, Taggart, is too many women and too much drink. You'd make a fine NCO if it were not for that. All right, I sentence you to ten days jankers...'

But at two o'clock on this cold March morning, Private Taggart was not fated to be 'crimed' yet once again. Instead, he found himself facing a pudgy-faced, balding politician, who he recognized easily enough from the papers. It was the same politician who had sent him to the Dardanelles, where he had been wounded for the second time, caught malaria and had been infected with a certain sexual disease by a bint in a Cairo knocking shop. That had cost him his first set of sergeant's stripes.

Now, after stuffing his false teeth into his mouth, he reached over for his wallet and said, 'Private Taggart – that is your name, isn't it?'

'Yessir,' said Taggart, standing stiffly to attention in the centre of the wardroom, watched by a group of stern-faced officers.

'I should like to thank you for your vigilance. You have probably saved my life.' Churchill grinned. 'I am sure, Taggart, that there are many people in London, who wouldn't be so grateful to you for that, however.' He opened his wallet and pulled out a large crisp, white five pound note. 'Here you are, my good fellow. Take it.'

Taggart's eyes bulged. He had never had so much money in his whole life. *Five quid!* That'd keep him in tarts for a month or more. 'Thank you very much, sir,' he answered smartly, and took the note.

Churchill nodded and Taggart's company commander bellowed, as if he were back on the barracks square, 'About turn, Taggart. Officer on parade. Salute!'

Taggart slammed down his boot, clashed his hand across his rifle butt and marched out.

Churchill's grin vanished. 'There is something amiss here in Germany, gentlemen,' he announced, as a mess steward brought him a drink, which he accepted, as if the steward never existed. 'These recent killings of our people and then this attempt which was obviously directed at me.' He turned and said to the big major with the green brassard of staff intelligence on his sleeve, 'Billingborough, I would like you to send a full report of what you find out from those two prisoners to you-know-whom in London.'

'Sir. Yessir. I'll see to it straightaway.' The big major went out and Churchill sipped his drink reflectively, staring at his pudgy face in the mirror opposite. Outside, all was quiet again. 'Years ago, gentlemen,' he said softly, stroking his glass, 'I went hunting in India with the Maharaja Gaekwar of Baroda. The Maharaja owned one of the first automobiles in India and I sat in the rear seat with the cheetah he used for hunting between me and its keeper.'

The staff officers listened, fascinated, yet wondering where this story in the middle of the night was leading. 'Finally,' he went on, 'we spotted a buck in the jungle. The car was stopped. The *Shikari* unhooded the cheetah, slipped his lead and he was off like a shot. Off he went after its prey. When we caught up with it, the buck lay on the ground looking up at us with a look of inexpressible anguish in its glazing eyes, its throat held in a vice-like grip by the cheetah. The *Shikari* waited for the poor animal to give its last agonized convulsion, and then the cheetah relaxed its hold. Thereupon the servant gave the cheetah its coveted reward – the bloody testicles of the dead animal.'

Someone exclaimed, 'I say!' Another young officer gasped and involuntarily let his hands fall to the base of his stomach.

Churchill didn't seem to notice. He was too wrapped in his tale of long ago. 'When the cheetah had satisfied its appetite, it allowed itself to be hooded and leashed with the utmost docility. As we left the scene of the killing, the sinister beast, having licked its bloody chops, settled down on the seat once more with ingratiating friendliness. I shrank away from it.' He paused. Suddenly that mild, bantering look that was always present on his face, even at moments of seriousness appeared. He looked around at the circle of puzzled faces in the yellow light of lantern and said quietly, very quietly, so that they had to strain to hear his words, 'Today when I think of the German people, I am strongly reminded of that cheetah of so long ago.' He shivered dramatically and finished his drink in one gulp…

TWO

A single, flaring gas jet lit the white-tiled mortuary, which was freezingly cold. The place was bare of any furniture save for a long steel dissecting table. Along the wall were the freezers in which the dead bodies were placed.

With a curt nod, the coroner of St Pancreas indicated the two white-clad attendants should open up the 'depository', as it was called.

Swiftly, they stepped forward to carry out their task. It wasn't every day that they had such important visitors as Professor Spilsbury and the man 'from the Foreign Office', with his ramrod-straight back and monocle.

They pulled open the drawer, emitting a cloud of icy air, and revealing the body. With a grunt they bent, lifted it out and placed it on the steel table. Spilsbury looked at the little nervous coroner and he said to the attendants. 'Go upstairs and get my electric fire. That should do the trick.'

Minutes later the heat from the single-bar electric fire started to thaw out the naked body, which the man 'from the Foreign Office' watched with a certain amount of fascinated horror. Steam began to rise from the limbs and there was a steady drip-drip from the yellow, stiff feet.

Now Professor Spilsbury, the most famous pathologist in England, began his examination. He pulled on rubber gloves and set his horn-rimmed glasses more firmly on the bridge of his big nose. As was his habit, as if his secretary were there taking notes, he talked aloud as he conducted the examination. 'Split lower lip ... grazed nose ... abrasions on the chin... Further abrasions on right breast ... finger marks.' He looked up at the man with the monocle and said in that pedantic manner of his, which had rattled many a lawyer in the Old Bailey, 'Clear indication she was attacked from behind and thrown to the ground.'

The other man nodded, but said nothing. But those who knew him – and there were very few people in the whole of the British Empire who were allowed to know him – would have seen that he was becoming irritated by the pathologist's slow and self-satisfied performance. For he was beginning to tap his wooden leg with his malacca cane: a sure sign he was losing patience.

Gently, Professor Spilsbury forced open the woman's legs, peered into her vagina, holding the lips apart with a spatula.

'Hell's teeth,' the man with the monocle cursed to himself, as he watched, 'what a profession – peering up dead women's insides – *disgusting!'* But he kept his thoughts to himself, as Spilsbury announced, 'Sexually assaulted with great violence... She was virgo intacta ... tear in hymen ... private parts heavily soiled with blood.'

The other man nodded. 'Our authorities in Germany thought she had been raped. Her underthings were found next to her. But what can you tell me of the cause of death and who may have done it, Professor?'

Professor Spilsbury said, 'tut-tut.' He did not like to be disturbed in his labours, even by such important people as the 'man from the Foreign Office', though he suspected the man with the monocle who had brought him here wasn't from that department. His language had been decidedly undiplomatic when their taxi driver narrowly missed running over a butcher's boy on his bicycle. It had been a flavour, more of the quarter deck.

Gently but firmly he rolled the dead woman over on to her stomach. Carefully, he searched the body, starting at the feet and working his way upwards. He grunted suddenly. 'Raped first,' he announced. 'Then buggered. Clear evidence of that – here,' he pointed with his gloved hand.

'I'll take your word for it, Professor,' the man with the monocle said grimly.

Next to him, the little coroner shook his

greying head. 'There's been some terrible types about since the war. The trenches brutalized so many of our young men. For instance, there's been a tremendous increase in this area of young men riding without lights. Quite blatant some of them, when stopped on their bicycles by the constables–'

Spilsbury shot him a baleful look and he shut up immediately. 'Naturally, I can only hazard a guess on this. Without a PM – er, post-mortem – I cannot be sure. However, my guess is this. The girl was felled from behind, raped and then buggered. After that, she choked in mud or something like that, where she lay unconscious. There are clear asphyxial haemorrhages on her cheeks and neck.'

'Poor girl, the poor girl,' the man with the monocle said softly, visualizing the scene that night: her man friend cruelly stabbed and thrown into the river, then the defenceless girl raped in such a bestial fashion and left to die all alone. She had never regained consciousness. There had been nothing the British Army doctors had been able to do for the pathetic, brutalized child.

'Hello, what's this,' Spilsbury exclaimed suddenly.

'What's *what?*'

Spilsbury didn't answer. Instead he tugged a magnifying glass from the pocket of his topcoat and held it close to the girl's bare right shoulders. For a moment he stared intently at the naked flesh, then he turned to the man with the monocle and beckoned him forward.

His wooden leg squeaking slightly, he did so and said, 'Well?'

'It is quite common in these cases of buggery,' Spilsbury announced, as if he were lecturing a class of respectful students, 'that the victim is held quite firmly by the shoulders. To prevent the victim moving around or squirming with the pain of the insertion. Oftentimes the attackers, thus, leave marks.'

The man with the monocle nodded his understanding.

'If you look closely, you can see the faint pink marks left by the attacker's grip on her left shoulder.'

'Yes, I can see them,' the man with the monocle said. 'They are the very mark of the beast.'

Professor Spilsbury made no comment. He had long given up questioning the morality of the attackers of the many murder victims that he had to deal with. All that concerned him was to find out the cause of death and, if possible, discover who had been the criminal. And he often quoted to his sometimes appalled students those lines from John Wesley: 'Ah, lovely appearance of Death, What sight on earth is so fair? Not all the gay pageants that breathe, Can with a dead body compare.' Thereafter, he always had a good chuckle at the looks on their young faces.

He focused the magnifying glass again, trying to catch as much light as possible from the single flaring jet. 'Now look at the victim's right shoulder.'

Obediently, the other man let his monocle drop by its cord and stared through the proffered glass.

'Again, you can see the marks of the attacker's fingers. Look – one – two – three – the thumb and forefinger fused together in four. But examine more carefully finger mark number three.'

The man with the monocle peered more intently through the glass. 'I can't see anything special about it,' he announced after a few moments, annoyed by the pedantic medic who was taking him through his paces as if he were some damned fourth-form schoolboy.

'Ah, because you are not trained to see everything.'

The man with the monocle was tempted to retort, 'If you knew what I'm *trained* to do, you old fool, you'd be damned well greatly surprised.' But he kept that thought to himself. Instead he asked, 'Well, what is it then?'

'The indentation of a signet ring. Some men, as you are aware, turned the crest of their signet ring to the inside of the finger. There,' he heightened the magnification of the glass. 'You can see the design or emblem. Look, hold the glass and I'll sketch it for you.' He gave that pedantic smile of his. 'I'm always very keen to get a sketch of the body and its position before the police take it away. I have often been complimented on my work by the authorities.'

'Pompous old sod,' the man with the monocle cursed to himself. Obediently, however, he held the glass while Spilsbury went to work with pencil and sketch-pad. Rapidly, he put an end to the sketch and held it up to the flaring jet so that the other man could see more clearly. 'Well what do you make of that?'

The man with the monocle jutted his jaw angrily. There the old devil goes again, treating me like a damned snotty-nosed schoolboy, he told himself. He stared, a little puzzled, at what looked like a crooked cross. 'Isn't that the Greek cross?' he asked hesitantly.

'Oh, it goes back further than the Greeks,' Spilsbury said scornfully, eager, as always, to show off his knowledge. 'We can trace its origins back to the cults of ancient India and Persia. In fact, it takes its name from the Sanskrit word *"svastika"*.'

'Svastika?' the man with the monocle rolled the word around his tongue awkwardly. Then it came to him in a flash. He had seen that crooked cross once before. Just after the war, the beaten German Army had set up mercenary regiments from demobilized soldiers. Armed to the teeth, these free corps, as they had been called, had cut a bloody swathe through those eastern European countries which had once belonged to the old German Empire. In particular, one free corps division had been dreadfully feared throughout eastern Poland. It had been General von der Goltz's so-called 'Iron Division', a ruthless mob of thieves, rapists and killers – and the soldiers of the 'Iron Division' had worn that same crooked cross painted in white underneath a skull-and-crossbones on their black coal-scuttle helmets.

The man with the monocle gave a quick gasp, his mind racing electrically. The bits and pieces of the jigsaw puzzle seemed to be slowly coming together. But he wasn't there yet. He'd have to get his skates on though. Since he had arrived back from Germany, Churchill had been breathing down his neck. The politician had even phoned him from Victoria Station as soon as the night train from Cologne had arrived – a clear breach of security – and ordered that something had to be done – *'this day'*, as he had growled down the phone.

'I shall carry out the post-mortem at my own hospital this afternoon,' Spilsbury announced, when the other man didn't speak. He turned to the coroner. 'Ensure that the body is sent over straight away.'

The little coroner opened his mouth to answer, but the man with the monocle beat him to it. Now he took his revenge. 'There will be *no* post-mortem,' he snapped, as if he were back on the bridge of the dreadnought he had once commanded, giving orders to some careless snotty. 'The poor girl has suffered enough. Let her body rest in peace.'

'But there *has* to be a post-mortem!' Spilsbury snorted. 'There has probably been a murder. The matter must be investigated on the basis of the medical evidence–' He stopped short. Opposite him the man with the monocle was tapping his leg with his cane and for the first time Spilsbury realized he had a wooden leg.

'Spilsbury,' the other man said harshly and slowly, 'understand this. There will be no post-mortem. The poor girl will be buried in Hampshire by her people and that will be the end of it as far as you are concerned. And that goes for you – and you, as well,' he indicated the coroner and the two mortuary attendants.

'But you can't do that,' Spilsbury blustered.

‘Oh yes I can, Spilsbury.’ The man with the monocle tapped the pathologist’s skinny chest with the silver knob of his cane, ‘I can do many things of which you know naught. But suffice to say at this moment, if you breathe a word of what you have seen this afternoon in here, I shall ensure that you shall spend a spell in one of His Majesty’s prisons to which you have sent many unfortunates yourself in your time.’

‘Under what pretext, sir?’

‘No pretext. You will be consigned under the Official Secret Act. Now good day to you.’ He turned and limped out, leaving Spilsbury, standing next to the dead woman, staring at his straight back deflated and utterly bewildered…

THREE

Somewhere on the land a foghorn sounded mournfully. On the shore itself seagulls called shrilly, like babies calling for their mothers. Everything was damp and dripping with the wet fog. It was a typical east coast 'sea rock', cold and bone-chilling. Standing on the wet deck of the *'Swordfish'*, Lt. Smith, known throughout England as 'Common Smith VC', shivered and cursed East Yorkshire yet again. As his second-in-command put it often, 'East Yorks, old chap, really *is* the arsehole of the world – and we, unfortunately, are right up it.'

Smith, forgot the 'sea rock', and concentrated on his front, trying to penetrate the rolling white gloom, as the *Swordfish* wallowed silently in the swell. Ever since the beginning of the year, freighters had been bringing timber from Murmansk in communist Russia and unloading it in Hull. The export of timber had become a very important source of foreign currency for the new masters of a bankrupt Russia. But they had also brought with them another export commodity which was not welcome to His Majesty's Government in London – *spies and agitators!*

Ever since the end of the war, London had been deadly afraid of Red revolution taking place in Britain, just as it had occurred in virtually every other European country. Britain seethed with discontent. Ex-soldiers who had discovered that their country offered them little after four years in the trenches; unemployed factory hands; left-wing intellectuals – there were scores of such groups who would join in any revolution which promised them work, hope, and a new way of life.

'The damned country's going to the dogs!' the Chief had snorted at their briefing in that mysterious rabbit-warren of a place in Queen Anne's Gate. 'But we're going to stop the buggers getting their way. The King-Emperor has not appointed me to this post in order to allow the country to slip into revolution, begad!' He had looked at the two young officers standing rigidly to attention in front of the big desk which had once belonged to Nelson, jaw jutting out like the prow of the dreadnought he had once commanded. 'I want one of those Red buggers nabbed, caught red-handed, sneaking into the country. Once we've got one of the treacherous swine, we can put pressure on Moscow. Understood?'

As one he and 'Dickie' Bird had snapped, 'Understood, sir.'

'Then get on with it,' he had barked, 'PDQ' which meant, as in all things with their impatient Chief, 'pretty damned quick.'

It had not taken the two young officers, who had been fighting the Reds ever since 1918 when young Smith had won his Victoria Cross, long to find out how the Russians infiltrated the country. Gold sovereigns had changed hands in some of the more seedy pubs along Hull's Hedon Road, frequented by Russian seamen. There, away from the prying eyes of the freighters' political commissars, they had told Smith and Bird how they hove to just off the mouth of the Humber to allow a ship's boat to carry an agent to the coast. In this way there was no risk of an agent being discovered by customs or immigration.

Last week they had learnt that the Russian freighters, the *'SS Moskva'*, had sailed from Murmansk and was heading for Hull with timber – and also an agent. The information was reliable and had been brought from a disgruntled Russian stoker at a cost of twenty sovereigns, or 'Horsemen of St George', as he called them, his red eyes lighting up when he saw the gleaming gold coins. Now, they patrolled the North Sea off the Humber estuary, waiting for the *'Moskva'* and its undercover passenger to arrive.

Two hours had already passed in the freezing fog and there had been no sign of the Russian ship, which would have to enter the shipping channel in order not to arouse suspicion. They stamped their feet, longing for a mug of steaming hot cocoa laced with rum, and peered into the grey gloom until their eyes hurt with the strain.

Twice Dickie Bird had said mournfully, 'I think we've missed him, old bean. You could run the *Titanic* through this peasouper and we wouldn't spot her. Let's get back to jolly old Withernsea and curl ourselves around some very large whisky toddys in the Commercial Hotel's snug.'

And twice Smith had replied, displaying the determination and steel which had won him the VC at Kronstadt, 'Not on, Dickie, just not on. They'll turn up like the proverbial bad penny, never fear.'

Now, when even he was beginning to despair, they began to hear the steady throb of engines going very slow, followed by the clatter of the davits being let out. Up on the bow of the fast motor-boat, Ginger Kerrigan sang out in his nasal harsh Liverpudlian accent, 'To port, sir ... craft to port!'

The two young officers, standing there with their mufflers tucked around their throats, brought up their glasses. At the wheel above, CPO Ferguson, the *Swordfish's* tough old bosun, who the crew maintained was so ancient that he must have sailed with Nelson, tightened his grip, ready for instant action.

Now the expectant officers could just make out a dark shape edging its way through the grey, rolling fog, an engine purring softly.

'Can you make out how many, Dickie?' Smith whispered.

'Can't, at the tiller ... just vague shapes, the rest,' Dickie Bird answered.

Hastily, Smith turned to hulking, fat Able Seaman Bennett, nicknamed 'Billy' after the famous rotund vaudeville comedian. 'Billy, close up the Lewis gun.'

'Ay ay, sir.' Bennett cocked the big, clumsy machine gun effortlessly with his paw of a hand, though to Smith he seemed to make a devil of a noise. 'Keep it down to a loud roar, Billy, will you?' he snapped.

'Sir.'

Now they waited tensely as the craft drew closer. Was it the Russians? Or some local fishing boat from Withernsea or Bridlington which had blundered into the maritime shipping lanes by mistake? Smith, his nerves tingling electrically, though in full control of himself as always at moments of extreme tension, knew there was only one way to find out. When the unknown boat was perhaps some twenty feet away, still shrouded with the same fog that covered the

Swordfish, he cupped his hands around his mouth and shouted, 'What boat are you?'

The man at the tiller reacted immediately. For the first time, he saw the sharp outline of the motor-boat wallowing in the trough. Now he pulled the tiller hard right and began to disappear back into the fog.

'Heave to!' Bird commanded desperately.

No response. The little craft kept on going.

At the wheel, CPO Ferguson didn't wait for orders. Time was of the essence. If they lost the little boat in the peasouper, they'd have a devil of a time finding it again. He jerked back the controls. The *Swordfish's* engines burst into throbbing, excited life. Ferguson urged her forward. In an instant the sharp prow was out of the sea and those on deck had to catch on to something to prevent themselves from overbalancing. She shot after the other craft, great wild white furious sprays of water curving up from her screws.

'There she is!' Ginger yelled and pointed to starboard.

Smith didn't hesitate. 'Give her a burst, Billy!' he commanded.

'Ay ay, sir!' Billy Bennett yelled back. He slapped the wooden butt of the Lewis gun into his shoulder, squinted down the thick, ugly barrel and pressed the trigger.

Tracer zipped in a lethal red and white

morse towards the fleeing craft. The slugs hissed angrily just above the heads of the men in the boat, but still the man at the tiller didn't stop; and Smith could see why. Looming out of the fog now there appeared the ship which had brought the Russians to this place – and there was no doubt that it was a Russian ship. At its stern hung the new flag of the Russian Republic, the red flag, complete with gold hammer and sickle, the flag of world revolution.

'The stinker thinks he can escape back to that old tub!' Dickie Bird cried above the roar of the Thorneycroft's engines.

'Then he's got another think coming!'

'But we're still outside the three-mile limit. These are international waters, Smithie,' Bird protested urgently. 'We're not entitled to stop anyone out here.'

'Let the Foreign Office worry about that. Give those smarmy stripe-panted twits something to do for a change. CPO Ferguson,' he yelled at the bridge, 'give her all she's got!'

'Ye'll burst the engines, skipper,' CPO Ferguson yelled back urgently. For the sandy-haired Scot with the incredibly wrinkled face dearly loved the *Swordfish* and every piece of machinery in her.

Smith ignored the remark. Now he could see the davits being lowered down the rusting sides of the Soviet freighter. A Jacob's ladder was also being unrolled midships. If the Russian could reach that before they reached them, they'd abandon their boat and scramble up the rope ladder. Then it would mean tackling the *Moskva,* and with the handful of men under his command, Smith knew that could be dangerous; he had no illusions about the Russians. He had fought them for too long now. 'Give 'em another burst, Billy!' he cried. 'And if you hit them – well, it's just too bad.'

'Ger on, yer big pudden,' Ginger urged, 'hit the gits!'

Billy Bennett squeezed the trigger once more. Tracer hissed angrily from the heavy machine gun. Up on the deck of the *'Moskva'* someone yelled something angrily in Russian and hurtled a black object at the speeding *Swordfish.* Next instant it exploded in a burst of threshing, foaming water just off the craft's port bow.

'Oh, I say,' Dickie Bird commented in that deceptively fruity upper class voice of his, which hid a will of iron, 'they are being a tiny bit naughty. They're throwing grenades at us.'

At the gun, Bennett cursed. Just at the very last moment, the fleeing craft had swerved and his burst had gone wild. Now the escapers were flinging themselves out of the little boat and were scrambling up the Jacob ladder like terrified monkeys. 'What shall I do, sir?' he asked, as another grenade exploded and the *Swordfish* rocked violently. Icy water swept over the deck and drenched them.

But it was CPO Ferguson who made the decision for them. The *Moskva* was looming up ever larger. He could see the patches of rust and oil on her plates too clearly. He was on a collision course. With an angry curse and a wild jerk, he hauled the wheel round. The *Swordfish* slewed to one side. For a moment her wireless mast seemed to touch the surface of the sea. Hastily, Smith grabbed a stanchion and cursed.

Ferguson throttled back at the engines. The *Swordfish* slowed down, barely moving now, while Bennett tensed behind the machine gun, waiting for orders to open fire again. But for the moment Smith was undecided what to do. Dwarfed by the size of the 10,000 ton freighter, there didn't seem much hope of tackling it with their three machine guns. Could he board her by bluff and try to find the agent or agents? He was certain that that had been the case. Why else had someone flung grenades at them? But what did the agent look like?

While he agonized, a small burly man in a leather coat, which he could hear creaking even at that distance, approached the rail. He put his mouth to an ancient megaphone and said, first in Russian, *'Stoi?* What you want with ship? Outside three miles limit, *boshe moi!*'

Smith bit his lip. He knew he had to say something, but what?

He tried to bluff the Soviet captain, 'You have an illegal passenger aboard, Master. Release him to me and you can proceed into the Humber.'

There was no reaction. Instead there was a whispered conversation on the deck of the Russian vessel and an impatient, frustrated Smith imagined that the captain was having the demand translated for him in detail.

Next to Smith, Dickie Bird said, 'I don't know how we're going to manage this one, old house.'

'We'll manage,' Smith answered grimly. 'The Chief needs bodies. He's going to get one – or two.'

The Russian skipper came back to the rail and peered down at the '*Swordfish*'. 'What ship you?' he demanded suspiciously. '*Davoi*, what nationality?' He surveyed the length of the blue-painted, streamlined motor boat, obviously looking for a flag. But the *Swordfish*, which officially didn't exist, for obvious reasons, though Smith knew that anyone who knew anything about naval craft could recognize her as one of the Royal Navy's high-speed motor torpedo boats which had fought throughout the war in the Channel.

He didn't answer the Russian skipper's questions. Instead, he snarled savagely. 'I have instructions to take off an illegal passenger, or passengers. Please hand him or them over and then you can get under way, Captain.'

'*Njet!*' the Russian said firmly, shaking his head to make his meaning quite clear. Down below in the big freighter the engines started to throb again and Smith knew the ship would be underway in a few minutes. *What the hell was he going to do?*

But suddenly and surprisingly the decision was made for him. In that same instant that he stared up at the defiant little Russian skipper in his squeaky leather coat, Sparks, the *Swordfish's* radio operator, popped his head out of the hatch, and said, 'Signal, sir. A most urgent. Got to report back at once. You and Mr Bird are expected in London at ten hundred hours *prompt!*' He emphasized cheekily, getting a charge at indirectly giving an order to the skipper.

Smith overheard the remark. His mind was elsewhere, the Russian forgotten now. He knew who had ordered them to London so urgently and what that entailed for the *Swordfish* and its picked crew of volunteers.

Opposite him Dickie Bird winked. 'Looks as if the balloon's gone up somewhere or other, old bean,' he drawled. 'Just hope it's in a warmer climate than the ruddy North Sea.'

Smith nodded, his mind too full to speak. They were going on active service again…

FOUR

'This way, gentlemen,' the old servant, in the rusty black tailcoat and old-fashioned wing collar, croaked. In the years since 1918 when they had first entered this mysterious building in Queen Anne's Gate, the servant had seen them many times, but as always his lined face was like a mask, revealing nothing.

He ushered them into the lift. It soared upwards noisily at high speed. They arrived at the same old passage, so narrow that a modestly fat man could never have passed through it. It was lit by two naked bulbs and, in the shadows on both sides, they could hear the rats scrabbling. Dickie Bird shuddered dramatically. He could never get used to this secret HQ; never shake off the feeling of apprehension whenever they entered the place.

The servant led them through a steel door onto a narrow iron bridge which led across the gap, linking the roof of the big Georgian house with that of its neighbour.

Again they entered another network of passages. Finally, the old man stopped in front of a door with no name on it or any indication of what its purpose was. He tapped and a hearty voice responded immediately. 'Come!'

He opened the door and Smith and Bird filed in.

A bluff, hearty major with a large moustache, a chestful of medal ribbons and the red brassard of the staff on his sleeve, rose to greet them, with 'Which one of you two chaps is Smith?'

'I am, sir.'

The major held out his hand. 'Give me the pleasure of shaking your hand, Smith. Tremendous VC you won when you sank that Red battleship or whatever it was at Kronstadt in '18. We all had a damned good chuckle in the mess when that newspaper-woman, dressed as a nurse, got into the dock where they were treating your wounds and got that quote from you – what was it again?'

Smith's handsome young face flushed slightly with embarrassment. The episode had rankled ever since. The damned woman, whom he had thought was a nurse, had asked with such sweet innocence that he had been completely fooled, 'I believe you are the fourth son of the Earl of Beverly?' He had nodded and she had said: 'Well, does that make you an honourable or something?' To which he had answered with a remark that he had regretted ever since,

'No, Miss, I am just Common Smith.' Next morning the name had hit the headlines and he had been 'Common Smith, VC,' ever since.

'So you must be Bird then?' The hearty major continued and stuck out his hand again. 'Now take a pew, chaps, for a few moments till the Chief's ready for you.' He beamed at them and indicated the half-filled bottle of whisky on the table in front of him. 'Fancy a stiff 'un? Don't be vague ask for Haig,' he chortled, using the whisky firm's advertising slogan.

They shook their heads. They were both too excited to find out what their mission was to waste time drinking.

The major seemed able to read their minds for he asked in that bluff, no-nonsense manner of his, 'Are you game?'

'Of course, sir,' Smith said quickly. 'Not much fun trying to catch Reds in the North Sea at this time of the year.'

'Don't expect so,' the major said, pouring himself a generous measure of whisky. He went across to the little sink in the corner and added a little water to the drink, staring at them in the mirror above the sink. To him they seemed the very best of the Empire's youth. Both barely out of their teens and handsome in a public school sort of way. But the VC on Smith's chest and the DSO ribbon on Bird's indicated that they were veterans and that they had seen plenty of action since they had left Harrow-on-the-Hill together to volunteer for the Navy.

He took a hearty drink of his whisky, coughed throatily and returned to his desk. 'Spect you want to know what kind of show you're getting into, what?' he snapped.

'Yessir,' they said in unison.

'It's the Huns. They're acting up again. You know how bloody-minded the Huns are? Well, they've been up to all sorts of nasty tricks in the Fatherland, especially against our forces of Occupation.' He took another drink. 'Got to be stopped toot-sweet, as the Froggies say.' Behind him, the little light above the double leather door began to wink a bright green. The major put down his drink hastily. It didn't do to keep his boss waiting. 'All right, the Chief's ready to see you now,' he said and rose.

He opened the two doors and barked, as if he were on some barracks square, drilling recruits: 'Lieutenants Smith and Bird to see you, *Sir!*'

They went in. The room was large but by some trick of the lighting every object in it seemed to appear in silhouette. A line of red telephones on extensions stood on the great desk which had once belonged to Nelson. To the right there was a smaller desk littered with maps, models of aeroplanes and submarines and a row of bottles which suggested chemical experiments. The evidence of scientific investigation always seemed to the two young officers to heighten the overpowering atmosphere of mystery, in this secret world up in the rooftops of Queen Anne's Gate.

They waited a little nervously, as the Chief, known to a few as 'C', the head of the British Secret Intelligence Service, continued to write. Over the chair behind him was slung the khaki tunic of a colonel in the Guards bearing the red tabs of the Staff, though he had been known to wear any uniform from that of a sub-lieutenant in the Navy to that of a general in the Royal Marines. Next to it was propped up his black Malacca cane with its polished silver head.

C was a small man, going bald. What remained of his hair was already grey. But his face was set and hard as he concentrated on his papers through a gold-rimmed monocle. There was no mistaking the air of authority about him, the most mysterious man, in the whole of the British Empire.

It was rumoured, for instance, that on one secret mission during the war he and his son had suffered a very serious accident just behind the front (some said on the German side of it). His son had been killed instantly, and C had been trapped by his leg underneath the overturned car. While the German

Uhlans on their horses had begun to search for him less than half a mile away, he had coldbloodedly sawn off his mangled leg with his penknife and had crawled to safety, trailing blood behind him on the snow, just in time.

It was typical of the many legends that surrounded his person. Was it an invention, a tall tale? But how else could a former captain of the fleet lose a leg while engaged in a desk-bound intelligence job?

He dropped his scroll pen, sprinkled some sand on the letter and then signed it 'C' in green ink, for at the headquarters of the Secret Intelligence Service only he was allowed to use green ink. He looked up and gave them a wintery smile with his lips moving as if worked by steel springs. 'Good of you to come,' he barked. 'Please sit down. Are you both well and fit?'

Even if they had not been, the two of them would not have dared to admit it. 'Yessir,' they said, again in unison.

'Good, you'll need all your strength for what is to come.' He peered hard at their faces and seemingly liked what he saw, for he barked, 'The spell in the North Sea has done you some good. Put some colour in your cheeks.'

'With not much success, sir, I'm afraid,' Smith said, a little crestfallen, as he remembered his failure of the previous day.

'No matter. That business will be taken care of in due course. Now I won't lecture the two of you. I expect you both read the papers and know how bad things are in Germany at the moment. We, the French and the Americans occupy half the country right up to the Rhine. The rest of the country is run by a socialist government in Berlin, which cannot act efficiently without the aid of the army, and you know just how reactionary and right wing the army has proved itself since its defeat in the war?'

The two of them nodded obediently and wondered where all this was leading.

'Meanwhile, there are paramilitary organizations springing up all over the place,' C continued in that no-nonsense manner of his, 'both right wing and left wing. Recently, one of these right wing organizations has started to make attacks on our Occupation forces in the general area of Cologne, the British Army's HQ. There's been a bad case of murder and rape on one of our people, plus a lot of sabotage of our equipment – and,' he paused significantly, 'last week the Huns tried to murder Winston Churchill while he was on a trip on the Rhine.' C noted their surprise and said quickly, 'Naturally we're keeping this strictly hush-hush and not a word of what I have just told you must ever leave this room.'

'Yessir,' they both replied.

'Now two of the Huns who tried to kill old Winnie were taken. Our intelligence johnnies questioned them closely and got nothing out of them – nothing of value, that is – until we sprung this upon them.' He held up a piece of paper with a drawing of what appeared to be a crooked cross on it. 'This design or emblem was taken from the poor woman who was raped and murdered. They call it a swastika. Ever heard of it?'

They shook their heads, a little puzzled.

'I'm not surprised. They call it a swastika – *Hakenkreuz*, in the Hun lingo. And it is the emblem worn by a new Munich-based right-wing group called the National Socialists. They started out as a very minor organization a couple of years back. Indeed, there were only seven founding members. But after they started to get money from rich right-wingers, these National Socialists began to expand rapidly and even more so when a rabble-rouser called Adolf Hitler took over the party. But,' he gave them a wintry smile, 'I'll let an old acquaintance of yours tell you the rest.' He jingled the bell. The bluff major opened the door and he said, 'Send in Major McIntyre now please.'

'Yessir.'

The two young officers had last seen McIntyre back in 1919. But the man who came through the door had not changed much since. He was a little greyer and was now a major instead of a captain. He was still a tough colonial!

He was a Canadian really, of Scottish extraction, tough and lean who spoke little and when he did he did so from the side of his mouth. He was the type who liked to let their fists do their talking for him or if necessary a revolver. Smith knew the type. They had volunteered to fight for the 'mother country' and those who had survived the slaughter of the trenches back in 1916/17 had been commissioned in the field, becoming temporary 'officers and gentlemen'. Not that McIntyre could ever have been mistaken for a gentleman. He was too angry-looking, truculent and tough for that. Still, Smith had always liked the cut of his jib.

McIntyre gave C a careless salute, and, nodding to the other two, said in a Canadian accent with an underlying Scots burr, 'Hello, you two.'

'You know Major McIntyre's job?' C said. 'He works *officially* for the British Control Commission in Germany–'

'Frigging Huns,' McIntyre snarled.

'*Unofficially* he works for us. Now, ever since the start of this year when the attacks on our forces on the Rhine commenced, McIntyre has been trying to find out about this National Socialist group led by Adolf Hitler, what their plans are and, above all, why they are directing their venom against us instead of the French, who, as you know, have just occupied the Ruhr and are much more hated than we are by Huns.'

McIntyre lit a cigarette without asking permission, blew out a stream of smoke and said, 'Because the Frogs shoot 'em if they catch 'em. You British are a soft touch.' He sneered contemptuously.

'I say, you can't go around shooting civilians,' Dickie Bird exclaimed, attempting a little humour. 'It's not allowed.'

McIntyre eyed him coldly, as if he were a particularly unpleasant form of life.

Smith, as impatient as ever when it came to a new mission, said, 'But what has all this got to do with us? After all we're sea-based.'

C looked across at the tough Canadian, smoking silently, eyes narrowed as the blue smoke curled up about his lean face. 'McIntyre, you're the expert. You'd better tell them.'

McIntyre took the cigarette from between his lips, as if he was reluctant to speak, and said slowly, measuring every word, 'This feller Hitler is planning some big incident in our Zone of Occupation. I don't know what.' He looked hard at the two younger officers. 'But I *do* know that Hitler is out to take over Germany…'

FIVE

There was silence now in the cobbled village square. In the light of the flaming torches held by burly Germans dressed in brown uniforms, McIntyre and Dietz, his little interpreter, could see the blood-red swastika flag hanging from virtually every house. These new National Socialists were obviously pretty strong in this particular Rhenish village, McIntyre told himself grimly.

Next to him, Dietz whispered, 'It's very dangerous, the thing we do, Major. If they catch us, they will not stop. They will be throwing us in the Rhine.'

The tough Canadian didn't take his hard gaze off the square. 'They have to catch us – *first,'* he said out of the side of his mouth.

A big Adler touring-car came bumping over the cobbles. The guards opened a path for it and the civilians crowded forward to watch the coming spectacle. McIntyre flung up his night glasses. A familiar face swept into the circles of calibrated glass. It was one of the most evil ones the Canadian had ever encountered. Framed by a high fur collar, it was small and soft, with thin lips that looked as if they might have been painted on it. But it was not the German's intense pallor that was unnerving; it was the eyes. They were hooded and dark, as if they had no depths at all, with an expression of boundless sadism.

'An old friend *Kapitanleutnant* von Horn,' he whispered, lowering the glasses, as the big open tourer parked opposite the rostrum on which he would speak.

Dietz shivered. He knew the reputation of von Horn, head of German Naval Intelligence. He was a sadistic pervert who would stop at nothing in his attempts to reunite Germany under the rule of some strongman who would make Germany great again as she had been before her defeat in the war.

McIntyre told himself there were 'no spots' on von Horn, as his ancient mother, long dead, when he had been a wee laddie back in the Gorbals had said. He was on to this man Hitler. It looked as though this new leader was going to get the support of the military.

'Er kommt! ... er kommt ... he's coming!' The cry rose from a thousand throats. Next to the rostrum, the drum major brought down his baton. The fifes and kettledrums blared into action, bashing out a Prussian march in full blast.

Slowly, a big black Horch was making its way through the crowd, brown-uniformed thugs hanging on the sides, looking aggressively at the crowd, ready to drop off immediately if they spotted a trouble-maker and knock the merry hell out of him.

'Heil ... Heil Hitler!' The cry was taken up everywhere; right hands were thrust out rigidly on all sides.

McIntyre's hard face twisted into a look of contempt. 'Frigging Jerries,' he whispered to himself as next to him Dietz, who had deserted from the German Army at the end of the war and had thrown in his lot with McIntyre, hissed, 'There he is – *Hitler!*'

The car stopped. The SA thugs dropped to the ground in a rough circle, hands on their pistol belts. A burly figure stood up. He was dressed in a shabby trenchcoat and breeches. On his head he wore what looked like a flying helmet and in his hand he clutched a long, leather dog whip. He flung up his own hand, bellowed *'Heil'*, and then with the band playing his favourite *'Badenweiler Marsch'*, he strode purposefully to the rostrum amid the wild cheering of the crowd.

He marched up the steps, watched intently not only by McIntyre from his hiding place but von Horn, who would soon make the decision for his own group whether they would support the Austrian rabble-rouser, who, a mere four years ago, had been a simple lance-corporal in the Imperial Army.

For what seemed a long time, Hitler just stood there, hands on hips gazing down at the crowd. Then as the cheering died away, he started to speak, his voice soft so that his listeners had strain to hear his words. He explained the events of the last four years: how Germany had been stabbed in the back by the Jews, the profiteers, the intellectuals of the Home Front. It was they who had lost the war, not the brave German Army fighting in the mud and blood of Flanders.

Within minutes he had his peasant and working class audience in his hands. Now, his face flushed and glazed with sweat, one lock of hair falling over his narrow brow, he launched into the attack. He stormed at his favourite enemies, the Jews and the Reds. 'Our motto shall be, if you will not be a German, I'll bash your skull in... We cannot win without a fight, a bloody fight... Those traitors in Berlin must go... Liquidate them and under strong leadership we can make Germany whole again ... great... The French, the Americans, they must be tossed out of great Fatherland... They have no right to be here ... letting their black soldiers rape our decent German woman ... suck us dry of our last penny in reparations so that the plutocrats, the Jews, in London, Paris and New York can sit like fat pigs in shit...'

Now his audience were sweating, too,

some of them staring up at the new saviour, who was saying what ordinary German folk thought, with rapt devotion. Everywhere, too, the brown-shirted guards had forgotten their primary duties. They, too, were held in hypnotic spell by the demagogue on the rostrum.

McIntyre knew his time had come. He reached into his pocket and released the safety catch of the .38 that he kept there. Then he pulled the rubber cosh out of his other pocket and strapped the loop around his wrist. 'All right, Dietz,' he ordered loudly as the mob cheered and whistled, 'they're just right. Get back to the old jalopy and start up the engine.'

Dietz looked apprehensive, not for himself this time, but for McIntyre. He liked the tough Canadian. The Major had been very good to him in their four years together, though he had been frightened half that time. 'Be careful, sir,' he warned. 'They are bad people when angry.'

McIntyre gave him a hard grin. 'So am I,' he said, then he was moving down the dark street to the right of the square, the noise of the crowd and the ranting of the orator instantly deadened. He had already picked the man he wanted. He had come with Hitler and wore the stars of an officer on his collar. Just before Hitler had left the car he had spoken to the man. McIntyre hoped that he was the senior man of the bodyguard, the kind of person who would pick up all the big shots' gossip.

Now he edged his way around the square by means of the backstreets, which were deserted as he had expected. He passed the onion-towered church. A man was standing morosely at the open door, perhaps straining to hear the speaker in the square below. He was wearing a priest's robes. *'Guten Abend,'* McIntyre said in his best German.

'Guten Abend, mein Sohn,' the priest answered. There was a sob in his voice. Perhaps he already knew his day was over. He had lost his flock.

McIntyre turned the corner. Now he came out at the back of the square. To his immediate front was von Horn's car. That monster had his back to him, listening intently to Hitler, who was ranting, 'The Treaty of Versailles was a fraud, a mere piece of paper which we will immediately tear into shreds once we have come into power.' Just behind it was Hitler's car. Most of the bodyguard who had come with him had pushed forward to hear what their chief had to say and were staring, just as fascinated as the rest, at the sweating, gesticulating man on the rostrum. Only the officer remained, leaning against the side door. Perhaps he had orders to do so, McIntyre told himself, to ensure no one planted a bomb in the

Horch. These days the party bosses, left and right, regularly bumped each other off like Chicago gangsters. He nodded his approval. The lone man and his evident unawareness that danger was on its way suited him fine.

McIntyre stole forward, one hand clutching the butt of the big revolver, the other the rubber truncheon. In the next few minutes he would use both. Fifty yards to go. This was the crucial moment. It was like in the old days in the trenches with the 'heavies' blasting hell out of the Hun positions. Soon they'd also know the 'heavies' would stop firing to avoid killing their own chaps. Then, when that happened, the attackers would make that last desperate charge for the enemy wire, hoping and praying that the Hun machine-gunners wouldn't recover and run to their deadly weapons.

He came up just behind the lounging SA officer. Up front, they were still chanting and cheering, Hitler was throwing himself all over the rostrum. Every eye was concentrated on him. McIntyre took one last breath. Then he stuck the muzzle of the revolver in the German's ribs – hard. The man started violently as if he had been stabbed.

McIntyre didn't give him a chance to shout out. He slapped him across the back of the neck with the club and commanded, '*Ruhe*. Don't shout. *Now.*' He kept the

German simple. It was always the best way. Long instructions confused the victim and at the same time gave him time to recover and shout out. He shoved the muzzle harder in the startled man's back. 'Move it!'

The suddenly frightened SA man 'moved' it.

They started down the darkened village street which led away from the square. To their front lights flashed off and on. It was Dietz with the car.

The big Canadian prodded the German harder. He stumbled into a run. Behind them there was a shot, followed an instant later by a shrill whistle. At the wheel, gunning his motor, Dietz swallowed hard. Had they been spotted?

McIntyre flung open the door. He shoved him inside and as he did so, he brought the rubber cosh down hard on the back of the man's shaven skull. He collapsed without a sound on the back seat.

'That'll keep the swine quiet for a while,' he said through gritted teeth, while Dietz's expression grew even more worried. 'Come on, let's head for the Rhine bridge.'

Dietz needed no urging. He swung the car round. Behind them they could hear someone attempting to start a car, turning the cranking handle with little success save a series of throaty barks of the reluctant engine.

He pressed the accelerator down hard. The little car shot down the dead straight road, the vineyards on either side whizzing by. Behind them the car started up and McIntyre told himself grimly they had been rumbled. Someone had spotted them. He took out his revolver and laid it on his lap in readiness.

Next to him Dietz gulped with fear and almost lost control. 'Watch the frigging steering wheel,' McIntyre snapped hurriedly, as the car narrowly missed going into the drainage ditch at the right side of the country road. He flashed a look in the rear view mirror. Yes, they were being followed all right. Two headlights, hurrying forward at speed, were after them. 'Hit the floor, Dietz,' he commanded. 'Don't spare the horses.'

The glowing needle of the speedometer started to rise. *Thirty ... forty ... fifty kilometres an hour... Sixty.* The little car was shaking at the seams.

But still the other car kept up and in the rear view mirror McIntyre could see there was another car behind it. It would be the one that had brought Hitler to the meeting. He frowned and wondered how long it would take them to reach the safety of the Rhine bridge. Once across it they would be in safety. There was the British Zone of Occupation and British Tommies would be guarding the far side. For he had no illusions about what would happen to him and Dietz if the Huns caught them. They'd be slaughtered and dropped in some remote ditch within the hour.

'Come on, Dietz!' he urged. 'They're gaining on us.'

The first car was. It was cutting down the distance between the two vehicles rapidly and McIntyre knew it was time to act. He had to do something. 'All right, Dietz!' he shouted above the snarl of the engine, 'try and keep her as steady as you can.' Without waiting to see if Dietz had heard, he leaned far out of the open side window, steadying himself the best he could. He took aim and fired. The slug howled off the road yards in front of the car behind. He could see the sudden spurt of angry blue flames where it hit the tarmac.

McIntyre cursed and raised the range. By now there were spurts of scarlet flame coming from the other car. They were firing back. He took aim and pulled the trigger. The big revolver jerked upwards. In that same instant a slug slammed into the back of their car. On the rear seat the unconscious prisoner was thrust forward by the impact and slammed into the back of Dietz's seat. But he had no time to look around. He was concentrating frantically on the road ahead, praying fervently they would spot the bridge soon.

McIntyre fired again. Suddenly the car behind them was slithering out of control all over the road. A moment later it overturned, effectively blocking the road behind them. One man got out. McIntyre could see him in the overturned car's headlights, running desperately for safety. He just made it. As he flung himself into the drainage ditch, the darkness was split by a vivid flash of angry light. A moment later the wrecked car was blazing fiercely and McIntyre sat back, body lathered in sweat, and breathed a sigh of heartfelt relief. Five minutes later they were rattling over the bridge to where British Tommies, all polished boots and blancoed equipment, were staring at the mud-stained, bullet-holed car in frank astonishment.

SIX

'The sawbones tried to patch the Hun up, but it was no use,' McIntyre said as they sat, listening intently to his story of the kidnapping and that night chase to the safety of the British Zone of Occupation. 'But he was grateful and he sang. He thought we were trying to save his life.' McIntyre shrugged and lit another of his cheap cigarettes. 'We didn't. He croaked.'

'But he did tell you something,' C interjected hurriedly, though he had been intrigued by the tough Canadian's story just as much as the other two.

'Yes,' McIntyre breathed out a stream of blue smoke. 'Some.'

'What?' they all asked eagerly.

'Well, first that this Hitler feller is going to make an attempt to seize power in Germany.'

'You said before that it would be some time in the autumn,' C prompted him.

'Yes, there'd been a meeting of all these Hun storm troop chiefs and it was agreed they would all converge on Munich around that time. Once they had taken over Bavaria, the rest of Germany would follow.

McIntyre took a drag at his cigarette, knowing that they were all hanging on to his words yet determined not to be hurried. 'The second important thing I got out of him was that just before Hitler's attempt to take over power, his people are going to have a crack at the occupation powers.'

C nodded his understanding. 'Yes, some coup in that area would make him and his fellows heroes in the eyes of the ordinary Hun,' he said. 'But which power did he say they had selected?'

'Well, as sure as hell it won't be the Yanks,' McIntyre sneered, with all the contempt that most Canadians reserved for their neighbours below the 49th Parallel. 'The Huns think nothing of them.'

'The French?' Smith ventured.

McIntyre shook his head firmly. 'As I've said before, the Froggies shoot people – and without too much yes and no either. No, it's going to be one of our people in the Zone of Occupation.' He shrugged. 'Perhaps a place even, an army barracks in Cologne. Possibly Army HQ at the *Hotel Dom.*' He paused and let his words sink in.

For a while there was no sound in the room, save the muted whirr of an airship's propellers passing overhead. Each man was wrapped in a cocoon of his own thoughts and apprehensions.

Finally C broke the silence with, 'Do you

think you would like to have another crack at taking this bad business a little further, McIntyre? I know it'll be damned dangerous. I am clear that you are probably a marked man by now over there in Germany.'

McIntyre shrugged easily. 'Sure,' he said, 'I've been living off borrowed time ever since Vimy Ridge. When you survive and every other feller gets killed all around you, I guess you tend to think that you've got luck on your side.'

'Good for you, McIntyre,' C said enthusiastically. 'You see, the government doesn't want to see Germany re-united under any sort of strong man. We need a stable Germany, of course, to stop the Reds in the east moving further into Europe with all that bolshevik rot of theirs – government by the masses, how dreadful!' He wrinkled his face, as if he had smelled something particularly foul. 'But, at the same time, we don't want a powerful Germany governed by some sort of fanatic throwing its weight about. We had enough of that with the Kaiser and we all know what that led to – the Great War.'

The three of them nodded their agreement.

'So we must not give this Hitler chappie a chance of upsetting the applecart. In particular, we must stop him carrying out whatever he intends for our zone of occupation, whether it is an assassination or some sort of terrorist attack on our installations like the Irish have been recently carrying out in that accursed country.'

'Frigging Irish Micks,' McIntyre said softly and to himself.

Dickie Bird grinned and said, 'I say, old fruit, you don't seem to like anybody, what?'

McIntyre looked hard at the young officer and Dickie Bird closed his mouth quickly. It seemed safer to do that. McIntyre was obviously a man who didn't have a sense of humour.

'So this is what I suggest,' C continued, making his decisions as he spoke. 'While Major McIntyre returns to the unoccupied part of Germany and tries to find out what this man Hitler is up to, as far as our people are concerned, I want you, Smith, to take the *Swordfish* and sail to Cologne. That will be your base. From there you will be able to stop any attempts to cross the Rhine by these National Socialists.'

'Bit of a tall order, sir, if I may say so,' Smith objected mildly, for his heart had leapt at the promise of an active command once again.

'Not so much as you might think, Smith. In our area of occupation there are only the bridges at Dusseldorf, Cologne and Bonn to be watched. The Army will take care of that.

So you are confronted with an area of the Rhine which is fifty miles long at the most.'

'I see sir,' Smith said, not altogether convinced, realizing that they were being sent on a very uncertain mission. They knew not what the target was to be, nor who would perform the deed, nor indeed what that deed would be.

But McIntyre was plagued by no doubts. 'If there's nothing else, sir,' he addressed C, 'I'll sling my hook.'

'Yes, I suppose it's all,' C answered.

'How will we keep in touch?' Bird asked the Canadian.

The latter gave him his usual cold, scornful look, the one he always reserved for upper class Englishmen – 'shits', as he called them to himself – and said, 'You won't. That's the short answer. The less people know of my whereabouts, the better. But don't worry. When I've got something, I'll contact you.' He put on his battered, stained khaki cap and set it at a rakish angle. 'Now I'm going to get me a Piccadilly whore. Just in time before I catch the night train to Cologne.' He gave C a careless salute and swaggered out.

C breathed out hard. 'Sometimes that man–' he began in exasperation, then calmed down. 'But you must admit that he is a very brave man. Knows his business. Hard as nails.' He dismissed the Canadian with a sweep of his hand. 'Now, his point about security is well taken, Smith and Bird. Undoubtedly the Hun will have spies in our Zone of Occupation. So you will only contact our authorities in an emergency. You'll wear civvies and naturally the *Swordfish* will have to be modified too.' He gave them a wintry smile. 'Can't have you sailing down the German Rhine armed with torpedoes and a quick-firer, can we?'

They returned his smile and Smith said, 'We can turn her into a sort of pleasure cruiser, sir. A lot of chaps have bought surplus boats since the war ended and turned them into floating homes – that sort of thing.'

'I say yes,' Bird said enthusiastically. 'We'll be rich toffs – English milords off on a jaunt to the jolly old Continent. Money to burn with one eye on the lookout for the charming little ladies of the *demi-monde*, what!' He smiled brightly at the other two.

'Don't be an ass, Dickie,' Smith snapped. And C said sternly, 'There'll be no money to burn on this show. But you will be given an appropriate slush fund to bribe the natives. All these continental Johnnies like having their palms greased.' He said the words as if they constituted a well-known fact.

C relaxed a little, if that energetic, stern spymaster could be said ever to relax. He looked up at the two friends as if he were seeing them for the very first time and told himself that they were the very best of Englishmen: the kind who had made the Empire and who would give their lives selflessly to maintain it. He sighed. If there were only more of the kind instead of this new breed of long-haired, so-called 'intellectuals' who were determined on the destruction of England's great heritage.

'Well, that's about it,' he said firmly and rose, the joint of his wooden leg squeaking audibly. He thrust out his hand again. 'I'd like to wish you God speed. Come home safely. England has a great need of chaps like you in these hard times.'

They took the hand, saluted and did a smart about turn. C's presence made people do things like that. They were on their way – to the unknown...

King's Cross station was crowded. There were huge groups of young sailors, lugging big white seabags, Woodbines stuck at the side of their mouths, caps perched on the backs of their heads in a most irregular fashion. Most of them were slightly drunk, but good humoured in the fashion of the British matelot. A fiery-faced three-striper, very drunk, was reciting loudly, *'There was once an old man of Leeds who swallowed a packet of seeds. Great tufts of grass shot out of his arse and his cock was covered in weeds…'*

Smith grinned and said to Bird, 'I hope that old boy is sober enough when he gets to wherever he's going or the *Master-of-arms'll* really give him hell.'

Bird nodded.

By now they were both transformed. The smart naval uniforms were tucked in brown paper parcels under their arms. Their place had been taken by two none-so-clean blue suits bought at a pawnbroker in Camden Town. On their heads they both wore greasy 'gor blimey' caps.

'You realize that we can't travel first class in this gear,' Bird had said when he had first seen himself in the flyblown mirror.

Now, eyeing the crowd of drunken sailors, groups of raddled whores and crippled beggars with their tin mugs and chestfuls of war medals, he said petulantly, 'But I'm damned if I'm going third class with this little lot. Could catch all sorts of nasty diseases.'

Smith laughed seeing his old friend shudder, as if he were already afflicted by some loathsome skin disease. 'All right, we'll go second class, if that'll please you?'

Grumbling still, Dickie Bird said it would.

They pushed their way onto the platform, through a company of kilted Scots, hard-looking regulars with bulbous red noses and the permanently tanned look of soldiers who had done long service in hot climates. A mere boy with a single pip on his shoulder and no medal ribbons appeared to be in charge of them and he was bellowing out orders in a high-pitched, affected voice, which the soldiers obeyed in a slow relaxed way. 'Good job they haven't been raising their elbows,' Dickie Bird commented, 'or I think his nibs over there – what a pipsqueak – wouldn't get away with it.'

Smith grunted something and found their carriage, occupied by a plump woman with a shopping basket placed carefully at her side. She eyed the two young men suspiciously and said in a 'refained' accent, 'I hope you realize that this is a non-smoker.'

'Yes, Madam, we do,' Smith said, his mind already on other things, 'and I can assure you we don't intend to smoke.'

She sniffed and said, 'Well, mind that you don't.' Then she turned her head and watched as the Scots started to pile into the third class compartments at the head of the train, watching their beefy naked thighs under the dangerously swaying kilts with obvious interest.

Suddenly, however, her attention was caught by another spectacle. A small procession of important-looking people were being ushered down the platform by the station master in a top-hat. Behind them, a convoy of porters was pushing mountains of luggage. The procession stopped at the first class. The station master doffed his top hat. A man in striped trousers and a morning coat went among the porters, who also took off their caps respectfully, as he passed each man a sixpence. Then came much stiff bowing and clicking of heels, as the Scottish soldiers began to hoot, 'Why yon folk is squareheads! The Huns are here, laddies. Why didn't they hang Kaiser Bill?... *Come on, why didn't they hang Kaiser Bill?*'

Smith and Bird watched, amused, as the little subaltern ran up and down the platform opposite third class carriages trying to shut up his old sweats with cries of: 'I'll have the lot of you on a charge when we get to Edinburgh... Stop that disgraceful barracking at once!'

But in the end, the only solution was for the red-faced station master to signal the guard to blow his whistle. He shrilled it urgently three times. Doors were banged shut. The steel wheels clattered on the rails. Steam rose. Slowly, the train started to pull out of King's Cross on its long journey to Scotland.

Five minutes later, a little man in a well-pressed suit of a continental cut opened the door of the carriage from the corridor, bowed slightly and placed his Gladstone bag on the rack. He flashed a gold-toothed smile at the woman, closed his eyes and promptly went to sleep.

Dickie Bird looked at Smith and mouthed the word, 'Hun?'

Smith nodded.

Half an hour later, lulled by the rocking motion of the train they were fast asleep, too.

SEVEN

They awoke with a start. A jolt, a sudden rumbling and the train started to slow down. Bleary-eyed, they looked out at lights from the houses on both sides of the line. Opposite them the little man in the continental suit opened his eyes and said, 'Please, where are we now?'

Smith squinted at the sign to his right, 'Grantham,' he said.

'Aach, Grantham, yes. Thank you,' the man said, as if it was important.

The woman picked up her purse and basket and tugging her skirt tightly to her stout body, as if she were afraid of having any bodily contact with the three men, she swept by them, with 'I hope you'll excuse me?'

'Of course, we will,' Dickie Bird said, with a wink at Smith, pulling his knees almost to his chin.

She sniffed and departed, while outside, as the train came to a stop, a porter shouted, 'Grantham... Five minutes stop... Grantham...'

Suddenly the Scots were pouring out of the train, heading straight for the shining lights of the station bar, almost overturning the trolley being dragged up the platform by a youth, crying, 'soft drinks, tea, coffee, sandwiches!'

Dickie Bird looked at Smith and licked his lips. 'No chance of getting a drink with that lot filling the station bar. What about a cup of tea? We can stretch our legs, too.'

Smith nodded and opposite them, the little man said, 'I will watch your luggage,' he indicated the two parcels of clothing on the rack. 'One can never too careful be.'

Dickie laughed and said, 'Yes, one can never too careful be. Thank you. Come on, Smithie, before the lad runs out of tea.'

Five minutes later, pushing their way through the Scots, who were goose-stepping past the German in the first class compartment and making rude remarks about the deposed Kaiser, they found their own compartment was empty. The little man and his Gladstone bag had vanished, but their brown paper parcels were safe on the rack. 'Not much of a watchdog, our little German friend. I suppose his boss must have called him to his own compartment,' Dickie said. 'Probably wants him to polish up his sabre or something.'

Smith grinned. 'Something like that, I guess. Come on Dickie, let's get a bit more shuteye. We've got time before we change at Doncaster for Hull!'

'Well said,' Dickie agreed. 'Snore on, MacDuff.'

Up in his first class compartment, *Kapitanleutnant* von Horn shut his ears to the angry ranting of the ambassador in the next one – *'a gross insult ... I shall have words with the Foreign Office about the behaviour of those brutish soldiers...'* and stared up at the little man who was standing rigidly to attention as if he were back in the old Imperial Navy. 'Well?' he asked in that deceptively soft voice of his.

'The device is in place, *Herr Kapitanleutnant*,' the little man answered, staring rigidly ahead. 'They got off at the last stop. I did it then.'

'Excellent,' von Horn murmured and the little man chanced a glance. Von Horn was almost an albino. His yellow hair was cropped to the scalp so that it looked as if he were wearing a yellow skullcap and he had no eyebrows above eyes that were the pale blue of a mountain glacier. His new master, the little man told himself with an involuntary shudder, had the face of a murderer.

Von Horn dismissed him with a wave of his hand. 'You will leave the train at Doncaster. There you will catch another train to Hull. A tramp steamer, *SS Hamburg*, is in dock. It will take you back to the homeland. In no fashion must you be seen to be associated with the ambassador's shooting party.'

'Jawohl Herr Kapitanleutnant.' The little man seized his Gladstone bag and, clicking his heels, departed.

Von Horn relaxed a little in his seat, eyeing the tourist picture of Scarborough on the wall opposite. *'Scarborough'* he mouthed the name and remembered that splendid day in 1914 when the battle squadron to which he had belonged had totally outfoxed the English navy. They had spent wonderful hours systematically pounding the seaside town with their heavy guns. Behind, they had left a pile of smoking wreckage.

In the next compartment, the ambassador was still ranting on about the behaviour of the 'English soldiers in skirts', as he called the Scots. Von Horn allowed himself a sinister smile. The ambassador was a fat socialist from Magdeburg: a Mecklenburg peasant who had been one of those who had stabbed Imperial Germany in the back in 1918 and had been given this post as a reward, although he couldn't even speak a word of English.

He sniffed. Soon, this new rabble-rouser, who was a peasant, but who had his heart in the right place, would put an end to the regime of those Berlin traitors. Then Germany would be respected once more: the most powerful state in Central Europe.

Then, with Germany's honour restored, he would have time for his hobby once again.

For a few minutes he allowed himself to indulge his fantasy: visions of the naked bodies of the svelte boys with plucked eyebrows, painted lips and delightfully mincing gaits he had picked up in Hamburg's red light district. What pleasure they had once given him! Now, as head of the North German Naval Intelligence Division, an organization which those damned Allies had banned, but which functioned all the same, he had devoted himself almost totally to the restoration of Germany's former glory. Occasionally he would have a young sailor in his quarters but he hadn't had a real love affair since Imperial Germany's defeat in 1918.

He forgot the beautiful boys and concentrated his mind on the problem at hand. The damned Tommies had somehow got on to the plot. They had probably made the SA man they had kidnapped talk – the English were mealy-mouthed – all that talk about democracy and 'fair play' – but they were a hard, brutal people. They could make anyone talk. Now those two arrogant swine, Smith and Bird, who had crossed him before, had to be liquidated before they could poke their long English noses into Hitler's intentions.

He sucked his thin, cruel lips. The English

authorities would probably think it had been an accident. There had been several similar cases in the *deutsche Reichsbahn*, the German Railways, over the last few years. A heating system linked to coal gas was always very tricky. But even if that damned Secret Service of theirs thought differently, what could they prove? He smiled to himself. Nothing, *absolutely nothing!* He relaxed even more and closed his eyes. Beneath him the wheels seemed to be singing that triumphant new song of the Austrian Hitler and his party.

*'Heute gehort uns Deutschland und morgen die ganze Welt...'**

Smith was dreaming. It was 1918. His skimmer was going in at a terrific rate, skidding over the water, it seemed, as the Red, artillery blasted away on the quayside. Searchlights coned on the bucking, vibrating little torpedo-boat as it skimmed over the waves at forty knots. Behind him on the bridge, the three-striper, carried away by the frenzied unreasoning blood lust of battle, was screaming. 'Try this on for size, you Roosian buggers!' and spraying the Red batteries with his machine gun. All was

*'Today Germany belongs to us. Tomorrow the whole world.'

noise, chaos and sudden, violent death.

A dark shape was looming out of the red gloom and fog. Men were running along its deck in panicked confusion. A quick-firer started blazing away. It was their target. 'Fire!' someone called far far away. The *Swordfish* leapt as the first one ton torpedo hissed from her bow. A second followed. The two deadly tin fish exploded right in the centre of the *Spartak's* huge length. There was the creaking and rending of tortured metal. *She was sinking ... she was going under!* They were sending the Soviet battleship to the bottom of Kronstadt harbour.

The huge Scot exploded into the compartment, kilt flying wildly. 'Yon wee officer's no too generous with his whisky!' He chuckled drunkenly to himself, seeing again the look of total disbelief on the young subaltern's face when he had seen his silver flask of whisky had been drained empty. The man had gone barmy, running to find his revolver, threatening to shoot the villain who had stolen his precious whisky. The Highlander chuckled, 'He'll no shoot Hamish Hamilton, dinna fash yersen!' he addressed the two civilians who were slumped in a deep sleep. 'Did ye hear that,' he bellowed, when they didn't react to his boast. *'Did ye hear that ye broken-down civvies–'* He stopped short and sniffed hard.

There was a funny odour in the compartment. 'Have ye no washed yer feet this day?' he demanded, suddenly feeling himself becoming dizzy. 'I've a heid like an ox. A wee dram won't knock old Hamish Ham–' He peered through half-closed eyes up to the rack.

There were two brown paper parcels up there. From both there came a thin white trail of what looked like smoke. But Hamish Hamilton, who had been gassed on the Somme in '16, knew instinctively it wasn't smoke. 'Gas!' he exploded, feeling a red veil of mist threatening to overcome him.

With hands that already felt thick and clumsy, as if they were enclosed in boxing gloves, he fumbled with the leather strap of the outer door. Somehow he managed it. It swung open dangerously. For a moment he swayed there, as if he might pitch to the ground. Fresh, cold air came streaming in. The red veil vanished. He grabbed the first parcel in one huge hairy paw and threw it out into the night. The second followed. Then he went to work on the sleeping, 'broken-down civvies'.

It was thus that the irate little subaltern found him, busy slapping the faces of two civilians who appeared to be reluctant to wake up despite the rather too hefty blows that Private Hamilton was administering to them. 'My God, Hamilton, what are you up to now? You're an absolute disgrace to the Gordons! Stop that immediately!'

'Dinna blether – *Sir,*' Hamilton, stone-cold sober now, 'gie us a hand, ye wee man. These two have been gassed. You take the one with the yellow hair and start slapping his face. He's coming round already a bit. I'll concentrate on this one. He's worse off!' He turned back to slapping Smith's face.

Five minutes later Smith came round to find himself staring up at a red-faced Scot who smelled strongly of whisky, his head ached and his cheeks stung where Hamilton had slapped him back into consciousness.

'Thank God, Smithie,' Dickie Bird breathed fervently. 'Thought you were a goner this time.'

Smith shook his head and next moment wished he hadn't. 'Not this time, but what happened?'

Between them, Hamilton and Dickie Bird told him and while a little voice at the back of his mind said grimly, 'you've been rumbled,' he forced a smile and, reaching into his pocket, brought out a sovereign saying, 'Thank you very much, Private Hamilton, it appears you've saved our bacon.'

Hamilton actually blushed and said, 'It was no big thing, sir.' All the same he accepted the gold coin quickly. Then he swung them a tremendous salute and marched out.

Behind him the little English subaltern shook his head in mock wonder. 'That man has a crime sheet as long as your arm. But brave. Won the Military Medal twice in the last show they tell me.' He looked at them, curiously noting the cultivated air and accent of the two civilians. 'I say, what are you two chaps doing travelling second class. Bit infra dig, what?'

'Slumming … seeing how the other half lives,' Dickie Bird said, his usual cheerful self again despite a splitting headache. 'The age of the common man and all that stuff, you know.'

'I see,' the subaltern said, somewhat puzzled. 'Well, I'll be getting back. Good night.'

'Good night and thank you very much,' Smith said and then as soon as he had closed the door behind him: 'Well, Dickie, it's obvious they're on to us. That little swine – if I could get my hands on his throat I'd wring it good and hard – planted whatever it was while we were out having that bloody tea.'

Dickie nodded, suddenly sombre. 'Looks like it, old thing.'

'Well, as soon as we get back to Withernsea, we're going to disappear. We'll find some little place where we can hole up – somewhere along that coast and do the refit, getting rid of the torpedo tubes and the like ourselves. CPO Ferguson knows the drill. Then as soon as we're finished we sail for Holland–'

'And down the Maas into the Rhine?'

'Exactly. I don't know how we're going to do it just yet. But we'll try to run across the German border at night, when their authorities won't be able to get a visual on us–'

He stopped short. A tall man, with his yellow hair cropped so short that it looked as if he was wearing a cap of gold, was passing in the corridor. With eyes that showed no interest, he glanced momentarily into their compartment. Smith felt an icy finger of fear trace its way down the small of his back. Never in his life had he seen a face so evil. With the sudden, absolutely one hundred per cent certainty of a vision, he knew that it was, too, the face of the enemy...

EIGHT

Staithes, on the Yorkshire coast, had proved ideal for the refit of the *Swordfish*. The cliff-top village of some 200 souls, mostly fishermen and their families, was very isolated. A post van creaked up the hills from Whitby once a day and there was a weekly bus to the Whitby market. This was the extent of the villagers' contact with the outside world.

Not that they wanted much contact. They were a superstitious, taciturn lot who didn't take to strangers easily. They were set in their own ways, which went back for centuries. Certain words couldn't be used because they brought bad luck to the fishing. Women were never allowed on board their little fishing cobbles because women always brought bad luck and when the mood took the fishermen they simply wouldn't sail. If asked why, they would reply, 'Because today we're not going out' and that was that.

The *Swordfish* had been anchored just around the bend below the cliffs on which the village was located and out of sight to preying eyes. Each morning, the crew sallied forth from the little inn at the edge of the jetty, which was the place's only form of entertainment, their bellies replete with a hearty breakfast of smoked haddock and fried mashed potatoes and as much strong tea as they could drink. Even Billy Bennett, the crew's glutton, was satisfied. 'They're a funny lot up here, the yokels are,' he was heard to say, wiping the grease off his chin with the back of his big paw, 'but they know how to feed an eating man some proper grub, that's for certain.' Then they would begin a hard day's work, getting the *Swordfish* ready for her voyage across the North Sea.

The tubes and the gun were removed first. On the night that the operation was completed, a discreet truck from Hull arrived at midnight when the petroleum lamps which lit the fishermen's cottages had long been doused. The tubes and gun were loaded as quickly and as silently as possible and taken away to the naval dockyard off Hedon Road in the port city.

Painting followed, while Ginger Kerrigan and Billy Bennett dismantled the mounts for the two Lewis guns and stowed them below. As Smith told Dickie Bird, 'In an emergency we can always use the Lewis guns without the mounts. Any flat surface will do the job almost as well.'

Now, as the *Swordfish* was transformed into a brilliant white in the early summer sunshine, bright bunting and pennants were strung along the superstructure to give the impression of a small pleasure cruiser. A day later, the post van from Whitby brought with it a large consignment of parcels addressed to 'Captain Shire', which was Smith's alias for the time of their stay in the little village.

That night in the locked 'snug', which the landlord had given to them for the duration of their stay for a 'small consideration', as he called it, the crew gathered after the evening meal to open the parcels. There were gasps, laughs and sharp intakes of breath as the men saw what they contained. There were white ducks and yachting caps, flannels, Oxford 'bags', multi-striped blazers that bore the colours of the older universities, even a selection of mufflers of white silk and foulards in dashing colours.

'There you are – take your pick.' Smith announced with a smile. 'We're off on a pleasure cruise – so we've got to look the part.'

CPO Ferguson's craggy face creased in a look of dislike. 'I'm no wearing yon gear,' he announced firmly. 'I'd look a real Mary Ann. It's no right for a chief petty officer in His Majesty's navy to wear the like o' yon.'

'Don't be a spoilsport, Chiefie,' Dickie Bird chided him. 'Really spiving togs! I say, I've taken rather a fancy to those Oxford "bags"!' He held up a pair of the grey flannel trousers with their huge flares. 'I think I'd cut a rather dashing figure in those.' He smiled inanely. 'I'd have to beat the ladies off me in those.'

Grumpily, CPO Ferguson allowed himself to be kitted out in white flannels and a pink shirt, but he resolutely refused to wear one of the white silk mufflers. 'I'm no havin' yon thing,' he persisted. 'Real Nancy-boy gear!'

On the fourth day of their stay in the remote Yorkshire fishing village, with the weather changing now from sunshine to a grim grey day with the cold wind howling in straight from Siberia, Smith and Bird locked themselves in the 'snug' and discussed their plans. Hunched over their charts, Smith said, 'I suggest we sail down the east coast as far as Harwich and from there set an easterly course for Knokke in Belgium. It's a bit of a Belgian holiday resort and there is a casino there. We could gamble a bit. It's the sort of thing holidaymakers on the grand tour of Europe would do, wouldn't they?'

Dickie Bird's face lit up. 'I say, do you think his nibs–' he meant C, '–would sub to a little flutter on the tables?'

'C's slush fund has provided us with five thousand in gold sovereigns. I think that should allow us to spend a few bob on gambling.'

Dickie whistled softly. 'Five thousand!

God, love a duck. That's a fortune. His nibs must think this is an important show.'

'It is,' Smith said, face suddenly serious. 'The point is that our government does not want Germany to go right with a strong government. We want no more trouble with the Huns this side of the 20th century.'

'You can say that again, Smithie.'

'From Knokke,' Smith continued, 'we sail up the Waal – here – till we reach the German frontier at Emmerich – here. As I've said before, I intend to slip through their customs and immigration at night. I've got passports with faked names for the crew and ourselves, but the less contact we have with the Hun authorities the better. Thereafter, we'll proceed down the Rhine till we reach Cologne. Cologne is a tourist town, so I'm sure we can tie up there for a few days without arousing any suspicions. Besides, we'll tie up on the British Occupied bank of the Rhine – just in case.'

Dickie nodded his agreement as the wind rattled the little windows of the snug and the coke-and-wood fire crackled and burnt in the sudden draught.

'If we find we're attracting unwelcome attention after a few days we can move on along the Rhine, perhaps to Bad Honnef – here.'

For once Dickie Bird was serious. 'You know, Smithie, it's all very vague, isn't it?

Without McIntyre we're pretty lost. I mean if he doesn't find out anything, we'd just be waiting for something to happen – reacting *after* the event, as it were.'

'Exactly, Dickie,' Smith agreed, looking worried himself.

'Let's cross that hurdle when we come to it, Smithie,' Dickie Bird said in the end. 'We're supposed to be going on a pleasure cruise, so let's get some pleasure from it – at least at the start.'

'Agreed. Now, talking of pleasure, what about having the men stand down when they come off shift tonight? They ought to have some fun before this new show starts.'

'Yes, all work and no play does make Jack a dull boy. But where will they have fun in this rear end of the world? Perhaps there might be an exciting spelling bee going on at the Methodist church hall?'

'Don't be a silly ass, Dickie. You know what the chaps want? Wallop and tarts, as they'd put it. There'll not be much of that here. I suggest we ring for a couple of taxis at the post office and ship them to – say – Scarborough. There's always something going on down there. There are plenty of pubs at least and lots of young factory girls from the West Riding out for a laugh!'

Dickie Bird's face lit up at the prospect. 'I'm not snobbish, Smithie. I don't mind mixing with the proles, especially if they've got big breasts.'

Smith laughed. 'I'm sure you're not. For a Harrow man, you're remarkably free of prejudice especially when it comes to the fairer sex. But you're not going. Neither am I. They're on to us. They know us. But the crew are anonymous. I think it's safe to let them go.'

Dickie pulled a face. 'I suppose you're right. I guess we'll have a high old time at the spelling bee tonight, what?'

CPO Ferguson saw them off, clad in their new finery and excited at the prospect of having a night on the town, with a contemptuous, 'Ye look a right bunch o' pansies. Mind yer don't bend down in them fancy trews or it'll be the worse for ye.'

Ginger Kerrigan minced into the taxi and blew the irate Scot a hand-kiss. 'Don't wait up for me chiefie, cos I'm gonna be the belle of the ball tonight. Coachman, take it away.'

Ferguson shook his fist at the crew's comedian and said, 'And mind ye's back by midnight or I'll have the lot of ye on the rattle.' With that, he stumped back through the rain and howling wind to the boat, where he was taking the first spell of the watch. Smith would follow him by midnight and at four, Dickie would relieve him. It was a duty they had taken on for themselves so that the men could sleep off their drunkenness without having to do a spell on watch during the night.

'Come on,' Smith said and shivered in the slick, gleaming oilskin, 'let's get back to the snug.'

'Yes,' Dickie answered, 'we must step out of these wet things, Smithie, and into a dry Martini.'

'Martini! They'll never have heard of 'em here. Let's compromise on a double pink gin.'

'I'm your man on that,' Dickie chortled. Thrusting his arm through Smith's, they hurried back to the comfortable, yellow-lit fug of the little inn.

Back on the *Swordfish*, CPO Ferguson settled down to his pipe, whisky and his Walter Scott, for he dearly loved the writer's romantic tales of Scottish history. As he had often remarked to his fellow CPOs in the old days, when he was still serving in the regular navy, 'Mind I've had women of most nations, and several animals as well, but ye knew, there's nothin' better than a good buik by Walter Scott!'

Outside the storm raged fiercely. Protected as it was in the lee of the cliff, the *Swordfish* skittered back and forth at anchor and shook every time the wind buffeted her. Not that that worried the old salt. He had started off his career in the Royal Navy's old sailing ships and had gone round the Horn twice before he was eighteen. He was used to worse storms than this.

Yet, he still could not concentrate totally. It wasn't the storm; it was that old Celtic sense of foreboding of his. It had been that same sense of foreboding – looming danger – which had saved him before the Battle of Jutland back in 1916. On the spur of the moment, he had changed watches with another petty officer. Thus he had been on the deck watch and able to fling himself over the side when the old ship had been hit by that first tremendous German salvo. Had he stayed with his original watch he would be trapped helplessly below decks like the man with whom he had changed watches. He had gone to his death with so many of his poor shipmates.

Finally, he gave in to the lurking sense of unease. He drained his malt whisky, grabbed his oilskin and a torch. He stumbled up the companionway. The wind howled and the icy raindrops lashed his craggy old face. He didn't notice them. Instead he moved slowly across the slick, wet deck shining his torch suspiciously from side to side, the knowledge that something was amiss growing on him by the second.

But nothing seemed out of place. The pots of white paint they had used to paint the *Swordfish* were still neatly stacked. The fake sail which they had rigged that day to lend credence to the cover story that this was a pleasure cruiser was still expertly furled. All was in order.

'Ach, ye silly old bletherer,' he said to himself, in the fashion of lonely men. 'Ye're na mair than a daft Jessie–' He stopped short. In a momentary lull in the howling wind, he caught another, strange sound. It was above him on the jetty. His reaction was very quick for such an old man. He flashed his torch up immediately. A small man in a long un-English-looking raincoat that came virtually down to his ankles was crouched there next to the pile of oil drums which they had used to fuel up the *Swordfish* that morning. 'Hey,' he challenged angrily, 'what's yer little game–'

Something flashed silver in the man's suddenly raised hand. Ferguson didn't hesitate. He flung the heavy torch straight at the little man. He yelped with pain. The knife clattered to the jetty. In that same instant, CPO Ferguson had hauled himself over the side. The little man still holding his hand, which was running with blood, backed terrified against the drums. *'Nicht schlagen!'* he shrieked with fear. *'Bitte – nicht schlagen!'*

'A bluidy foreigner, eh. Well, tek taht!' Ferguson hauled back his fist and slammed it right into the little man's terrified face. He went flying backwards, scattering the oil drums with a hellish clatter, unconscious before he hit the wet concrete.

NINE

Dawn!

Outside the storm had abated. To the east the sky was beginning to tint a faint pink. The sea was glass-calm, green and unruffled. It promised to be a nice day.

A weary Smith hoped it would be, for after what they had learnt this long, very long, night, the *Swordfish* would sail as soon as everything was ready and – and that wouldn't be long. The crew, most of them hungover, were already busy about their duties under the supervision of jubilant CPO Ferguson, proud of his capture of the previous night. 'Ay, wiel,' he kept reminding them of how he'd knocked out the little German, 'ye mind I was the Fleet's middleweight in the old days.' And even Ginger Kerrigan's snide comment, 'Yer mean under Nelson, Chiefie?' didn't put him off his stroke.

Smith and Bird had recognized the unconscious man, as soon as Ferguson had dragged him into the snug, trailing water all over the polished floor. Despite the bloody face and the broken nose which was already beginning to swell rapidly, they had both exclaimed in unison, 'It's him – the little man on the train at Grantham!'

Without the slightest scruple they had rifled through his pockets, found the German passport with its eagle stamp, and a round metal badge the size of a half crown with a long number stamped on it and the word 'Kriminalpolizei', which they reasoned meant 'criminal police'. 'Something like our CID,' Bird said. 'Funny kind of CID though – trying to kill two handsome innocent types like ourselves!' He had laughed, but there was no merriment in the sound.

An hour later two heavy, plodding constables and a sharp-eyed little plain-clothed detective had arrived to take the man away for further questioning. For, although there were no charges they could prefer against him – he had done nothing criminal – C, in answer to a hurried phone call, had ordered the German to be detained at His Majesty's pleasure, which meant the local police would be able to hold him until the big boys from the Special Branch got to work on him.

But, in the meantime, helped by Ferguson's constant threatening look, they had done their inexpert best to get what information they could out of the terrified, still bleeding prisoner. He was indeed a detective, but a very special one, it seemed.

By now they had given him a drink and a

cigarette, and with a handkerchief, red with his own blood, clutched to his broken nose, he explained. 'In the war I was no good for soldier.' He tapped his skinny chest with his free hand, and coughed. *"TBC".*'

Smith nodded, 'Consumption.'

'*Ja, ja, Tuberklosis.* So I became detective for Colonel Nicolai. Like your secret service.'

It appeared that during the four years of war he had worked as a detective for the wartime head of the German *Abwehr,* blackmailing, shadowing suspects and probably indulging in bits of petty thuggery here and there also.

Now there was no German secret service – officially – and he had begun to work for a *Kapitanleutnant* von Horn of the banned Naval Intelligence organization. 'Very bad man,' he had exclaimed with some vigour. 'I fear him.' The man he described as his new boss was the man with the cropped skullcap of yellow hair that Smith had glanced at in the corridor and known instinctively to be the enemy.

'Look,' Smith had said, as the window panes rattled in the gale and the petroleum lamp had flickered, casting their shadows against the walls of the snug, 'I'm ready to see that after a time you are quietly deported with no charges laid against you. There might be some money in it, too.'

'Money, yes, I understand,' the little man said eagerly, still trying to staunch the flow of blood.

'What did this von Horn fellow tell you about us?' Smith continued.

'Not very much. He tells things only to his boys. You understand. He does this.' He thrust the tip of his thumb between his two other fingers, the continental gesture for fornication.

Dickie Bird whistled softly, 'You mean he buggers boys?' he exclaimed.

The little man didn't understand the phrase. Instead he said, 'Ja, Ja, Homosexuell. But he did tell me that he has fought against you in the Baltic and in the – er *Mittelmeer.*'

'–Mediterranean?'

'Yes, before, and that you are bad men, very important English spies. You must be liquidated before you can cause trouble in Germany again – this year.'

The cross-examination had gone on a little longer, but had produced little else of importance, save that this von Horn had become a friend of the new right-wing rabble-rousers in Munich.

Now this dawn, with the sun beginning to slip a bright, blood-red over the lip of the sea, both Smith and Bird knew that their mission had been virtually compromised from the outset. Still, Smith was determined to go ahead with it. 'We don't want swine like this von Horn chap and his cronies to take over in Germany. Then we'll be back to the bad old days before 1914 with the Huns throwing their weight about all over the place. The country's got to have a chance of becoming a democracy.'

'Agreed, old bean,' Dickie said, 'though sometimes I think Europe would have been a happier place if Germany hadn't existed at all, but no matter. Look at it like this: So the Hun has twigged us. What can he do?' Dickie answered his own question. 'In Dutch waters nothing, at least *officially*. There'll be a bit of a problem at Emmerich on the Dutch-German frontier, but with a bit of luck, we can pull it off. Once we're in the Rhineland, we stick to the left bank, occupied by our own forces.'

Smith considered a few moments, his harshly handsome face set and tense. Outside Billy Bennett was singing in a highly untuneful bass, *'Never bin done, queen of all the fairies, isn't it a pity she's only one titty to feed the baby on...'*

'I'm ready to have a go, Dickie. But I'm not risking the chaps' lives without their approval. They're a rough-and-ready lot, but they're the salt of the earth, too. I'm going to put them in the big picture and ask them what they think.'

'Good idea.'

A few minutes later Ferguson had 'stood the men to', and Smith was telling them what he knew. 'I think we're up against that chap and his hirelings who tried to wreck the *Swordfish* in France last year. Now we know that he's a Hun called von Horn, something big in their intelligence and, I must add, an absolute swine who will stop at nothing, including cold-blooded murder.' He looked grimly around the circle of their faces, but if he expected to find fear or apprehension on them, Smith was disappointed. They remained, as always, attentive, interested, calm.

'Well,' Smith went on, 'I feel I must tell you this, lads, this von Horn chap knows we're coming. How we will do it, he *doesn't* know, but as I have said, he knows we're off to Germany for this coming show. Now I want to put this to you. In view of the fact that we've already been rumbled and this snake von Horn is highly dangerous, do you want to go ahead with it?' Swiftly he added, 'I won't take it amiss, if you say no. I value your courage and past loyalty too much for that. Well, what do you say, chaps?'

CPO Ferguson shot a hard look to left and right, as if he suspected there might be some waverers. He was wrong.

As one of the crew said, 'We're on, sir! No squarehead is gonna frighten off the good old *Swordfish!*'

Smith beamed at them, feeling that old warmth for these men of no education and with few prospects who were prepared to risk their young lives for a pittance. 'Thank you,' he said thickly, so much moved that tears shot into his eyes.

Ferguson turned on the crew. 'Well, come on,' he snorted, 'don't just stand there like a lot o' old biddies, gossiping afore the dramshop. Get back to yer jobs.'

Cheerfully, whistling and joking, as if they hadn't got a care in the world, the men trooped back down to the jetty and their last few tasks on the *Swordfish.*

Four hours later they were on their way, plodding through a calm sea, sailing close to the coast, heading southwards, and still in sight of the land, each man on watch carrying out his duties in a quiet, routine manner, but without the usual banter common on board ships of His Majesty's Royal Navy.

Smith felt the mood. It had always been like this, he knew, when they were setting off on a show. Suddenly, it seemed, the men realized that they might be leaving the Old Country for ever.

'Penny for them, Smithie?' Dickie Bird asked softly, as they stood together on the bridge, eyeing the flat mudbanks of the Lincolnshire coast.

'The usual at these times,' Smith answered, equally softly, pointing to the coastline. 'Doesn't look much does it? Mud, cliff, soggy fields and a few scruffy cows. But it's England – *our* England.'

'I know what you mean, Smithie,' Dickie said, unusually serious for him, his normal bantering, affected tone vanished. 'There's no place like it in the whole wide world, is there?'

'You can bet your bottom dollar on that,' Smith said with sudden enthusiasm, his mood vanishing as quickly as it had appeared. 'God, to think that that little island rules over one third of the world. All that red on the map! A while back this morning I had my doubts about this show. Not now. We British have always triumphed in the past, come what may. We'll do it again now.'

'Of course, we will, Smithie,' Dickie cried, infected by his old friend's sudden change of mood. 'We'll show those bloody Huns who's top dog. Now then, we can leave the helm to dear old Chiefie here–'

CPO Ferguson shot Bird a look, but said nothing. In all his years of service in the Royal Navy he had never got used to the strange ways of officers. They were a breed apart.

'–And go and tuck ourselves around a large pink gin in the wardroom. We're going to celebrate.'

'Celebrate – what?'

'The new show, you deuced ass. Come on.'

Grinning like schoolboys, suddenly released from boring lessons, they went clattering down the steps towards the ward-room, while up on the prow a suddenly happy Billy Bennett began to sing: *'And the mate at the wheel had a blood good feel of the girl I left behind me...'*

They were on their way.

BOOK TWO

THE PLOT THICKENS

'Wooden eye – stay alert.'

Old German Saying

ONE

They took Dietz at midnight.

Half an hour before he had seen the signal, the light being switched off twice in rapid succession. That meant her husband had gone to his job on the night shift at the post office. She opened the backdoor, looked sharply to left and right, and within minutes they had been writhing and twisting on the sofa in the 'best room' under the disapproving gaze of her elderly husband in the photograph on the wall above the sofa.

Dietz wasn't a passionate man, but Klara, as she was called, was well endowed and had been deprived. It was she who took the initiative. Now, with her legs tucked around his skinny neck tightly, the sweat pouring off her naked body, she was gasping, 'Albert... Just a bit longer...' When the door burst open and there they stood.

Four of them. Big men dressed in leather overcoats, dark hats pulled well down over their foreheads, no expression on their lower faces.

Klara didn't even scream. She couldn't. She simply collapsed on the rumpled sofa, as the leader of the intruders tapped Dietz on the skinny yellow rump with the silencer of his pistol, saying in a low voice, 'All right, the fun's over. You're coming with us.'

'But where?' he managed to gasp, knowing that the game was up already. He had been a damned fool to cross over to the other side of the Rhine to have his fun with the neglected suburban housewife. McIntyre had always warned him about it. Now it had really landed him in the shit, as McIntyre would have said. 'Are you the police?'

'Don't ask questions – just get dressed,' their leader said in a voice devoid of emotion. Dietz could see he wasn't even interested in Klara's ample charms, as she lay there in sweat-glazed confusion, her legs spread widely.

Almost sadly Dietz got to his feet and reached for his long woollen underpants with the buttons at the back. He pulled them on slowly, his mind racing, wondering if there was any way out of the mess he had got himself into. But after a moment's consideration, he realized there wasn't. The window was tightly shuttered and one of the men in leather coats was standing in front of the door. He started to pull on his shirt.

The leader spoke to the woman. 'Stop that racket!' he said sharply. 'Pull yourself together and don't say anything of this. Or your husband will find out what his darling little wifey does when he's away working at night. Clear?'

Suddenly Klara realized she was naked in front of four strange men. She closed her legs sharply. One hand went to conceal her breasts, the other to cover her pubic hair.

'Did you hear me, bitch?' the leader snarled, suddenly losing his temper. 'Answer me!' He slapped her hard so that her face slammed against the pillow.

'I hear you,' she said and began to cry softly.

'Good. Now remember what I've said. Now you,' he turned to Dietz, who suddenly was overcome by an overwhelming fear, as he realized abruptly just how dangerous these men were. 'Get a move on. We haven't got all day.'

Fingers like clumsy sausages trembling with fear, Dietz threaded the stud through his collar and wound his tie around his skinny neck. A minute later, he was outside in the deserted street. The leader whistled. At the end of the road, car headlights suddenly flicked on. A car motor started and a new Mercedes, all gleaming paintwork and polished chromium lamps, came rolling smoothly down the street towards them.

'Get in,' the leader ordered sharply and gave Dietz a push, which sent him flying into the back seat. A moment later the big black car was speeding away into the unknown...

'Permission to speak, *sir?*' Sergeant Hurt was an old sweat, but he was a guardsman, too. Now, after ten years of service and four years in the trenches, he had not lost his old Brigade of Guards' habits. He slammed his right foot down hard and stood rigidly to attention in front of McIntyre's desk.

The Canadian winced. 'God Almighty, Hurt,' he complained, as he had often complained before, 'must you be so damned regimental?'

Hurt, whose keen blue eyes seemed to be fixed on a spot known only to him somewhere in the far distance, snapped, 'No sir. Trained like that, sir part of the system, sir.' Hurt always talked in short, staccato phrases.

McIntyre gave up. 'All right, stand at ease and speak.'

Hurt's right foot shot out and he slammed his ammunition boot to the floor, placing both arms behind his back. 'Dietz didn't report for duty, sir. This morning, sir. Should have been on at eight hundred hours, sir. Didn't turn up, sir.'

McIntyre sat up. The Canadian didn't like Germans on principle, but the little ex-deserter from the Kaiser's army had been very useful to him as both an interpreter and a spy. 'That's funny,' he said slowly. 'Those Huns are a pretty punctual bunch as a rule.'

'Yessir.'

McIntyre scratched his head. 'What do you make of it, Hurt?'

'Don't know, sir.' Hurt had learned in ten years of service, never to volunteer opinions, especially to officers. That way, you avoided trouble.

'Jerry bint outside, sir. Dietz's bit o' stuff, sir. She's crying, sir. Can't make head nor tail of what she's saying, sir. She might know, sir.'

'Bring her in, quick.'

'At the double, sir!' Hurt slammed his boot down with tremendous panache and again the Canadian winced.

Moments later he returned, ushering in a large, full-breasted woman with fading blonde hair, who looked red-eyed, as if she had been crying a lot. 'The woman, sir.' Hurt announced.

'I can bloody well see she's a woman,' McIntyre snapped. 'All right, wait outside in case I need you. I'll deal with it.'

'Sir!' Again Hurt slammed down his boot, executed a smart about-turn and marched out, swinging his arms shoulder-level as if he was back on guard duty outside Buckingham Palace. McIntyre sighed like a sorely tried man.

A few moments later McIntyre had managed to calm the woman down and now in his halting but understandable German he began to ask her what she knew. He didn't like speaking German, just as he didn't like most Germans, but Dietz had been a loyal, if fearful, subordinate and he was determined to find out what had happened to him from the woman.

'I don't care if my husband finds out,' she sniffed, 'but I loved Albert. He was so kind and understanding. Every time he came he always brought me a little gift.'

Looking at the big buxom woman and recalling just how small and skinny Dietz was, McIntyre told himself cynically, old Dietz would have needed more than a 'little gift' to please this modern Brunhilde. Aloud, he said, 'But what happened?'

Hurriedly, interrupted now and again by a little sob, she told him, adding, 'At first I was shocked and frightened. Then I pulled myself together. I wasn't going to let them take my Albert away from me just like that.'

McIntyre leaned forward eagerly. 'So what did you do?'

'I rushed to the door and took the number of the Mercedes car.' She patted her shabby brown handbag. 'It's in here. But really to find it you don't need the number.'

'How do you mean?' McIntyre asked hurriedly, for he knew the German police authorities on the other side of the Rhine wouldn't co-operate with the Allied occupation powers; they would never trace a car number for them.

'Well, my husband works for the post office,' she answered. 'He is very methodical. Tells me lots of boring things and I have to listen, though sometimes he drives me to distraction. More than once–'

'–Please, go on,' he interrupted her.

'Well, the number starts off with a "K". That's for "Koeln".'*

'Yes, I understand. So it's a local car.' His face fell. 'But Cologne is a very big place.'

'I know. But the next letter is another "K" and there is only one area of the city with that number. I know it from my husband.'

'And what's that?'

'Koeln-Kalk. A poor area. There won't be many Mercedes in that part of the city, believe you me, Mr Officer.'

McIntyre sprang to his feet and crossed to the big map of the headquarters city. The Rhine neatly divided the city in half. There was a whole number of different districts on the other side of the great river. Hurriedly, he ran his forefinger across the map, muttering the names as he did so, *'Koeln-Mulheim ... Koeln-Delbruck...'* There it was *'Koeln-Kalk'* to the south-east of the city, on

*Koeln is the German name for 'Cologne'.

the road leading to Bonn.

He sat down again, mind racing, while the pale-faced blonde stared at him in pathetic hope. Finally she could stand the silence no longer. 'You will bring my Albert back to me, won't you?' she cried. 'I do love him – and I don't care who knows it.' She looked as if she might burst out crying again at any moment, her bottom lip was quivering mightily. Hurriedly, McIntyre brought out a packet of twenty *Woodbines*, worth a small fortune on the black market. 'Here take these. Sell them off. Get yourself a taxi back across the bridge.'

She rose and before he could stop her, she had taken hold of his hand and kissed it. 'Thank you, Mr Officer ... I thank you from my heart. I know you'll bring back my Albert.' She turned and swept out, still muttering about her 'darling Albert', leaving the tough Canadian to stare in wonder at his hand where she had kissed it. In all his life no one had ever kissed his hand; no one would have *dared!*

He shook his head like someone trying to come around after a heavy sleep. He wasn't going to abandon Dietz, he told himself. At the same time, if he could find the men who had kidnapped him, it might well be the breakthrough he needed. His mind made up, he called, 'Sergeant Hurt! Sir!' Hurt stamped in and stood rigidly to attention.

Irritably McIntyre waved for him to relax and said, 'You've got civvies, haven't you, Sergeant?'

Hurt looked at the officer cagily. The soldiers of the Occupation Army were forbidden to wear civilian clothes in Germany, but most of the regulars had them. When they went out with the local girls they didn't want to be spat upon or abused the resentful local citizenry. Hence, most of them secretly purchased a suit on the black market for a tin of cigarettes or perhaps a couple of pounds of coffee beans. 'Why do you ask, sir?' Hurt queried hesitantly.

'Because, Sergeant Hurt, I want to take you and a handful of good men over to the other side of the Rhine. We can't go over there in uniform and there might be a bit of a rough house, too.'

Sergeant Hurt's hesitant look vanished. Indeed, he positively beamed at the words 'rough house'. 'Yes, I do happen to have a suit, sir,' he admitted.

'Good,' McIntyre was businesslike. 'Do you think you could find me half a dozen good men in the sergeants' mess who have civvies and wouldn't object to a dust-up?'

Hurt's grin broadened. 'I could find yer half a hundred, sir,' he answered enthusiastically. 'There's lot o' the lads who like to teach the squareheads another lesson. Cocky bastards.'

Five minutes later, six NCOs were standing at ease in front of McIntyre's desk, while he surveyed them. They were all old sweats, in their late twenties or early thirties. All of them bore the ribbons of the Great War on their chests and all of them had that tough, yet restrained, cheerful look of a good non-commissioned officer. McIntyre, not a man given to easy praise, liked the look of them and he said so, adding, 'The problem, then, is to find this black Mercedes motor car. It will lead us to the chaps who are holding my assistant. You'll have coshes and I have asked the Quartermaster to issue you with revolvers.'

They looked impressed and Sergeant Corey, a red-haired Irish Guardsman with the ribbon of the military medal on his chest, said, 'I haven't shot a squarehead since 1918, though I've been sorely tempted since we first came to Cologne.'

There was a murmur of agreement from the others. All of them had been subjected to abuse in the occupied city and there had been several physical attacks on men who had ventured into the red light district after dark and on their own.

'Naturally, I don't want the firearms to be used unless it's strictly necessary,' McIntyre said, his tough face hardening, 'but if these fellers, whoever they are, pull a gun on you, you fire *first*. My experience has always been that even the professional might hesitate to shoot. They think of what might happen to them, to their careers, to their families. It might only be a fraction of a second from when you notice the tightening of their jaws until they decide to fire, but that's got to be *your* fraction of a second. Understood?'

They nodded their shaven heads, suddenly very grave at the thought of what might soon be expected of them.

'All right. Go and get your civvies. I've got a truck and driver waiting outside HQ. We'll change under the canvas cover at the back. In we go as soldiers, out we come as civilians.'

Smartly, they clicked to attention, did an about-turn and left, leaving McIntyre to rub his jaw reflectively, as he realized that if they didn't find Dietz this day, he would be dead by nightfall. He was certain of that.

TWO

'You treacherous little swine, *you will talk–*' the leader of the four men who had kidnapped Dietz slapped him across the face once more. Dietz' battered head rocked from side to side, a new wave of pain hurrying electrically through his skinny body.

They had roughed him up right from the start. He had expected that. At first he had thought the four kidnappers might have been men hired by Klara's husband to put a fright into him. But he had soon realized they weren't. They were out to discover what his boss was up to. Their questions had been very obvious. 'Why are you working for the damned Tommy?... What does he do?... Do you know anything about the kidnapping of an SA leader last month...?' They had rained the questions down upon him, slapping and punching him all the time until both his eyes were puffed and reduced to slits and his thin face was swollen and black-green with bruises.

In vain, he had protested time and time again. 'But I'm only his clerk and interpreter, *meine Herren* ... I know very little about what the Major really does. It has never interested me.' But each time they had not believed him and the blows had started once again.

By now it was fully light. He could see that through the chinks in the curtain which covered the windows and he could hear the rattle of the trams outside taking the workers to their factories in the city. He had reasoned they were still in Cologne – their journey in the Mercedes had been very short. He had reasoned, too, that if he did tell them what he knew about McIntyre and his current mission, he wouldn't live long. His torturers would want no witnesses and they could hardly keep him imprisoned for ever. No, coward that he was, Dietz told himself, the longer he kept his secrets, the longer he would survive. Besides Dietz believed passionately that McIntyre would somehow find and rescue him.

Now, above the clatter of the early morning trams outside, Dietz could hear the sound of running water coming from the next room. Why were they allowing the taps to run, he asked himself dully. For his usual nimble, quick mind seemed to be working awfully slowly. He peered through the slits of his eyes. Two of his kidnappers were absent. He concluded they were the ones who were running the water.

He dismissed the matter. It wasn't important. What was important was that for the time being they weren't beating him. Now he had time to think. He had to make himself think. In time, he knew, they'd make him talk. First of all he had to make them think they were winning. He had to appear weak and willing. The weak part wouldn't be difficult. He *was* weak. But willing he wasn't.

So what was he going to tell them when it appeared they had beaten him into co-operating? It had to be nothing about this upstart Hitler and the missing SA leader. That would be the end of it for him. It had to be a totally different 'confession'. But what?

'Hey you, traitor!' The sharp voice commanded harshly, breaking into his thoughts. 'On your feet and come here.' It was the man at the door.

Behind him, the other man in the little room gripped him by the hair and tugged hard so that he screamed with pain and pulled him to his feet. 'Obey orders, you crap-arsed piss pansy.' He let go of Dietz's hair and propelled him to the door with a hearty kick on the rump. Dietz slammed into the wall next to the door. Even in his fear and pain, he noted that the water had stopped running in the next room.

'Well,' the man at the door said, taking the cheap cigar out of his mouth and pressing it routinely to Dietz's left cheek. There was a smell of burning. Again Dietz screamed. 'Well, are you going to spit it out? Or do you want more of this, arse with ears?'

'But I know nothing, sir,' Dietz quavered, tears streaming down his ashen face with the pain of it all.

'Lying swine!' The man at the door opened it and, in a sudden fury, grabbed Dietz by the scruff of the neck and flung him inside. Again he slammed painfully against a wall and slid down the white tiles next to the big bath. He closed his eyes and pretended he had fainted. Anything to give himself a few minutes respite.

The one they called Klaus, the leader, kicked him in the stomach. He gasped with shock and Klaus sneered, 'Enough of that faking.'

With little effort, because he did feel terribly nauseated, Dietz started to vomit, allowing the sick to spurt down the front of his blood-stained shirt. Klaus jumped back hurriedly.

One of the others laughed. 'Nearly had your boots there, Klaus,' he commented.

'Shut your shit trap,' Klaus snorted angrily. He looked down at the man slumped in the corner, retching. 'Not only are you a traitor, but you're a filthy pig, too. *So eine Schweinerei!*' He spat down at Dietz.

The gob of spit hit Dietz on the face. It didn't matter, he told himself. It was all part and parcel of the interrogation: a calculated attempt to humiliate him.

'Well, we'll soon make a cleaner swine of you,' Klaus said. 'All right, get a hold of the bastard.'

Strong hands lifted him. He felt himself raised bodily from the corner. One pair of hands held him by the feet, the other by the scruff of his neck. He opened his eyes. They were holding him above the bath full of water. Was it hot? Were they going to scald him to death? The terrifying thought shot through his brain. Then he realized that no heat was rising from the water. It was cold. But what *were* they going to do to him?

Next moment he found out.

'*Jetzt!*' Klaus rasped.

With all their strength the two men holding Dietz plunged him deep into the bath. He was caught completely by surprise. He opened his mouth to scream and found it filling with water immediately. Stars started to explode before his eyes. His ears popped. *He was drowning!* Desperately he struggled and squirmed, a great roaring threatening to overcome him. But he was held in a grip of iron. He knew he was dying. One more moment and he would be gone.

Suddenly they let go. He dragged his head out of the water and slumped with his arm hanging over the edge of the bath, sucking in huge gulps, his skinny chest heaving frantically.

Klaus looked down at him contemptuously. 'Had enough?' he demanded, while behind him one of the kidnappers guffawed and said, *'Himmelherrje!* Have a look. The filthy swine just gone and shat himself! What a hell of a stink!'

'Schweinehund!' Klaus slapped him hard across his wet face.

Dietz didn't care. He was still trying to get his breath back.

'In again!' Klaus commanded. 'Clean the swine up first.'

The other two picked him up again, looks of disdain on their slablike faces. He struggled wildly, trying to kick out with his feet. To no avail. Down he went once more, the man holding his face beneath the water with a paw held to the back of his head.

Once more everything went red in front of his eyes. He choked and gurgled, feeling his lungs fill up with water. His ears popped alarmingly. They were going to kill him this time. He hadn't a chance. He was dying.

Suddenly, startlingly, the iron grip was released. Blindly, sobbing like a broken-hearted little child, he hung over the side of the bath, dripping water and fighting for breath, his chest heaving madly, as if he had just run a great race. They looked down at him unfeelingly, their tough faces showing no emotion in the yellow light of the single bulb, except contempt.

Klaus waited a few moments. Then he barked, 'Now, I'm sick of you. Next time you drown. All right, are you ready to tell me the truth now?'

For a moment, Dietz couldn't speak. All he could do was to nod his head weakly.

'Endlich,' Klaus said. 'High time, too. All right get him out of the damn bath.'

The two toughs hauled him out and dropped him on the floor, where he lay huddled and sobbing in a pool of water and his own dirt.

Klaus gave him a savage kick in the ribs. *'Los,'* he cried. 'Let's not waste any more time.'

'Can I clean myself up first?' Dietz quavered, still fighting for time.

'Heaven, arse and cloudburst!' Klaus exploded. 'Oh all right. Give him some shit house paper ... over there.' He turned and lit a cigarette.

With fingers that felt as if they were encased in clumsy boxing gloves, Dietz undid his flies and pulled off his trousers, then his soiled underpants, trying not to see his bleeding, bruised legs. He accepted the roll of pink crepe lavatory paper from one of his captors, his face set in a look of absolute loathing and disgust. Slowly he wiped himself clean and stood there with the soiled paper in his hand looking puzzled.

'For God's sake, *Mensch!'* Klaus roared, face red with fury, 'put the stuff down the crapper. God, you make me sick.'

Slowly, painfully, Dietz tottered across the bathroom and did as he was ordered.

'And pull the damned chain!'

Klaus dropped his cigarette and stubbed it out angrily on the floor with his shoes. 'Now, talk. What does your chief know? What's he up to. Did he kidnap the SA leader at the meeting when Hitler spoke? *Dalli, dalli* – Answer!'

'Well,' Dietz commenced slowly, hoping that they would accept what he answered, then suspect it and begin all over again. It was the only way he could gain time. If he couldn't, he'd be a dead man before this day was out, 'not very much. He knows – or thinks he does – that this Herr Hitler is intent on taking over power in Germany–'

'–When?' Klaus snapped.

'He doesn't know that.'

'Go on. What else?'

'He thinks that there might be some sort of an attack on the Allied Control Commission,' Dietz said hesitantly, selecting his words with care, 'or Allied soldiers.'

'Why?' Klaus shot at him, his face showing just how interested he was.

'I know not. He hasn't told me,' Dietz quavered.

Klaus looked at the other three and then asked very deliberately, 'Does your chief know if there is any connection between Herr Hitler and this supposed attack?'

Dietz shook his head, keeping his head lowered, avoiding eye contact with the big man. The question was again confirmation that this Hitler was mixed up with the plot to launch some sort of an attack on the British. But what role did his kidnappers play in it all? Were they members of Hitler's Nazi Party or were they something else?

'You haven't answered my question,' Klaus said menacingly. 'Indeed, I don't think you're altogether telling the whole truth, you little shit–' He broke off suddenly. 'What's that?' he hissed, cocking his head to one side.

'What's what?' one of the others blurted out startled. 'I can't–' His words ended abruptly. The door below splintered and broke as a sledge-hammer slammed at it.

'We're in trouble!' Klaus yelled in alarm. 'Get a hold of him.' He indicated Dietz, hand dropping to his pocket where his pistol rested. 'Come on. They're after us!'

Down below there came the sound of heavy boots. Someone hissed a command. Klaus recognized the language. 'Great crap on the Christmas Tree,' he cried, pistol in hand, now, 'It's the shitting Tommies.' Wildly, he looked around the bathroom for some means of escape. 'The window,' he cried. 'Get that shutter down. We can drop into the garden below. *Los!*'

Frantically, as Klaus faced the door, pistol in hand, the others ripped and tore at the wooden shutters that sealed off the little bathroom. Outside a voice said, 'They're in there!'

Klaus didn't understand English, but he recognized the tone. The damned English knew where they were.

He slipped off the safety catch. Face set and taut, he aimed and fired. The noise was ear-splitting in the confines of the tiny bathroom. Outside somebody yelled angrily. Klaus could hear the intruders fling themselves to the floor for cover. 'That's stopped them for a minute,' he cried. 'Now hurry up with that damned window!'

With one last desperate heave, the two men at the window pulled down the shutter. Klaus didn't hesitate. He wrapped two towels around his left arm, still carrying the pistol in his right, and smashed the arm against the window. It splintered. Glass flew everywhere. Hurriedly Klaus clawed out the remaining fragments and then yelled, 'All right, let's go. You,' he pointed the pistol at Dietz, naked save for his shirt, 'you go in front of me. No funny business either. *Los!*'

McIntyre, watching from behind the shed,

grinned coldly. 'Here, they come, Hurt. No unnecessary shooting. I want the sods alive.'

Hurt crouched next to him, pistol in hand, nodded. 'Pity, though, a great pity.'

'Shut up,' McIntyre snapped tersely, as the first man landed on his feet, and crouched there, gun at the ready. The others followed. McIntyre gasped. There was Dietz falling out of the window, his shirt billowing out about his naked bloody, tortured body.

'Well, I don't know what that big blonde sees in him. That ain't much to write home about,' Hurt whispered and chuckled.

But McIntyre wasn't listening. He straightened up and broke cover, big automatic levelled. *'Haende hoch,'* he snapped. *'Mach kein Theater!'*

Klaus gasped. His jaw hardened, as if he might press the trigger of his pistol. McIntyre beat him to it. 'I wouldn't if I were you, chum,' he snapped. 'Just look behind you.'

Klaus swung round. Four hard-looking men had risen from the bushes, weapons at the ready. They were trapped. He let the pistol drop to the grass. A moment later, the others were doing the same and a weeping, smiling Dietz was kissing McIntyre's hand deliriously, crying over and over again, *'Thank you, Major … thank you!'*

'Christ,' McIntyre exclaimed in apparent disgust, 'that's the second time this day that somebody has kissed my pinkies. I must be doing something wrong… All right, let's get back to the bridge before the cops arrive…'

THREE

'Dordrecht,' Smith announced as they started to thread their way through the traffic in the busy Dutch port, heading for an anchorage. 'We'll spend the night here. Any instructions from C will, apparently, be waiting for us at the main post office *"poste restante"*.'

'Good show,' Dickie Bird said amiably, eyeing the docks, where lines of buxom girls in wooden clogs were busy gutting and cleaning gleaming silver herrings which they threw into great barrels of brine.

Next to him at the wheel, CPO Ferguson growled: 'I've been here before in 1912, showing the flag. So I can tell ye what they do with yon herrings. They eat them *raw.*' His craggy face broke into a look of disgust. 'Worse than yellow chinks with them rotten eggs of theirs.'

Dickie Bird grinned. 'Oh Chiefie, come off it. You've been everywhere and seen everything, yet you're the worst bigot I've ever met.'

CPO Ferguson said, 'I dinna ken what yon big word means rightly, but if it means I don't like furreigners, then you're dead right, sir.'

Slowly, they lined the *Swordfish* up against the long jetty, which seemed to run the length of the estuary, watched by a few bored waterfront types in baggy trousers tied at the ankles most of whom wore a kind of fur hat on their heads; all were smoking white clay pipes in silent contemplation. 'Slow both,' Smith ordered and then a moment later, 'Stop both.' The *Swordfish's* engines went dead and they glided the last few yards in silence until they bumped gently against the jetty wall.

At the bow, Billy Bennett, holding the stout rope, cried in English, 'Hey, one of you lot, grab a hold of this!'

One of the watchers took his pipe solemnly out of his mouth, tapped out the dottle, blew in the ball, thrust the pipe in his pocket and walked very slowly over to Billy Bennett, who said, 'Don't rupture yersen, mate.' He threw out the hawser. The man caught it in the same unhurried way and tied it around one of the bollards.

That task completed, he held out his hand and said in English, 'One guilder, please.'

'Well, I'll be blowed,' Billy Bennett exclaimed. 'Fancy wanting money for *that*.' All the same, he hauled out a piece of the Dutch money, with which they had all been supplied, and tossed it to the solemn

Dutchman. He caught it neatly, bit it, then raised his fur hat. A second later, he sauntered back to the rest of the silent, sombre onlookers.

'Cor ferk a duck,' Ginger Kerrigan commented, 'Ain't they a bleeding lot o' laughs. I bet a sailor could have a fine old time in a place like this.'

'Well, as long as they've got something with chips in it, I'll be satisfied,' Billy Bennett said, his big stomach already beginning to rumble in anticipation. 'I'm bleeding sick o' bully beef and spotty dick.'

'Christ, can't you think of nothing else but grub?' Ginger snorted. 'Ain't you got no time for the finer things o' life?'

'Such as what?' Billy asked puzzled.

'Beaver, fer instance? I ain't parted no beaver for so long, I've almost forgotten how to do it.'

Up on the little bridge, CPO Ferguson was also concerned with the same problem, namely 'beaver'. 'Are you gonna let that bunch o' randy men ashore, sir?' he asked Smith as the anchor rattled to the bottom of the estuary.

'Well, I thought we could let half a watch go this morning and the second half this afternoon. I want everyone on board before it's dark, however.'

The old Scot tugged the end of his nose, thickened by years of salt winds and copious drams of his beloved Scotch. 'I was thinking ye would, sir,' he commented. 'But ye ken there could be a muckle trouble. There's plenty o' cheap hussies in a place like this – and plenty of yon diseases, ye know what I mean, sir?' He hinted darkly.

'Have a heart, Chiefie,' Dickie Bird moaned, eyeing the ample bottom of one of the bonneted girls cleaning the herrings, who had bent down in her broad starched skirt to reveal a plump, knickerless bottom. 'There's not much pleasure in this life for a poor sailor man. He's got to have *something.*'

'Ay, I ken that wiel, sir. But the price he pays sometimes is awful high.' CPO Ferguson sighed. 'Wiel, so be it, sir. But dinna say I didna warn ye.' With that he stalked off, muttering darkly to himself.

Smith shook his head in mock wonder. 'I've often heard it said, Dickie, that the English take their pleasures sadly, but God knows I've never met anyone who takes them as sadly as the old Chiefie. No matter. All right, I'll see off the first half of the watch and then find the main post office for C's instructions. You're in charge of the afternoon watch...'

'Rightho, Smithie,' Bird said happily. 'Give me time to spruce up a little. Bit of the old pomade and talcum powder, you know.'

Smith looked at him. 'You are going to run

those terrible risks old Chiefie has just outlined, Dickie?' he asked with mock pomposity.

'You bet your life, I am, Smithie,' Dickie answered joyfully. 'I shall find myself some beautiful lady of the night and indulge myself in absolute, unadulterated bliss. Spiffing!'

Half an hour later the morning watch was assembled, dressed in their new finery, their faces clean and shining, eyes sparkling in anticipation. Smith looked at them. 'Just one thing to say, lads. Stick together.'

'What – in between the sheets, sir?' Ginger Kerrigan asked cheekily.

CPO Ferguson shot him a murderous look, but Smith said mildly, 'No, I think that would be taking it a bit too far. All the same, stick together and don't get lost. You've got four hours. Get on with it.' He stepped on the jetty and headed for the solitary horsedrawn cab further up the quay. With a whoop, like excited schoolboys being let out of the classroom after a long day of boring lessons, the half watch headed for the brothels, while the other half looked longingly after them before heading below to the 'ablutions', as the Navy liked to call the greasy tin bowls in which they washed.

The cabbie stopped outside the *Centraal Post*. Smith paid and dismissed him and reached for his passport. He strode inside. The place wasn't very busy. A man leaned against a pillar reading *De Telegraaf;* an old woman comforted someone else's crying baby ensconced in a strange high pram made of wickerwork, a yellow man lazily cleaned the littered floor. He threaded his way through them to the counter marked *'post restante'*.

A prim-looking clerk in a black jacket and pince-nez stood there. 'Dag,' he said in a bored manner, like someone who had been doing the same boring job for too long and resented the fact that he had.

Smith took out the fake passport with which C had issued him and opened it in front of the man. 'Post for Mr Owen?' he asked in English.

The clerk no longer looked bored. *'Engels?'* he asked, looking at the name and photograph. *'Ja ja.'* He went to the row of pigeon holes at the back of the little office, peered along it and selected a letter. *'Hier.'* He thrust it at Smith.

'Thank you,' Smith said and walked away to the far end of the concourse. He looked at the envelope. He noted it bore a Dutch stamp and had been posted that very morning in Dordrecht. He nodded his approval. C was being very careful. He had sent whatever message the envelope contained by radio and in cypher to the British

CPO* in the British Embassy at the Hague. The latter had decoded the message and had driven down to Dordrecht that morning to post it. Thus, instead of going through innumerable hands the letter had gone through those of the CPO alone – and, naturally, the counter clerk.

He slit the envelope open carefully and unfolded the message. There was no letterhead, date or any other clue to the sender. The note was brief and to the point. It read: 'New developments in the B.A.O.R.' For a moment Smith was puzzled by the initials, then he remembered what they meant – 'British Army of the Rhine'. 'Report to our friend at the Cathedral for further instructions soonest.' There was no signature.

Again he was puzzled by the 'Cathedral'. The friend was, of course, McIntyre, but 'Cathedral?' Then he got it. The HQ of the British Army of the Rhine was located in the former German *Hotel Dom* – and *'Dom'* was the German for 'Cathedral'. He nodded his head and told himself that McIntyre had obviously found out something new since he had left London. The news cheered him up. Now they had something to go on. He stuffed the paper into his pocket and

*Chief Passport Officer, the cover for C's agents throughout the Continent.

strolled out of the big echoing station into the bicycle-filled streets, where it seemed the cyclists competed with the tram drivers on who could make the most noise with their bells.

Behind him at the counter, the prim-looking clerk nodded. The man reading *'De Telegraaf'* nodded. With seeming casualness he folded the paper, put it under his arm and strolled out into the sunshine after Smith. Contact had been made.

'Cor,' Ginger exclaimed as the two of them entered the waterfront brothel, filled with drunken sailors though it was not yet midday, and saw the prostitutes sitting on wooden chairs along the far wall. All of them were skimpily dressed and all of them had their legs well spread to reveal they wore no knickers. But it wasn't that which caused Ginger's surprise. It was the sheer size of the women. They were all huge, some nearly six feet tall, with massive breasts bulging from their cheap frocks. Great flanks and bellies quivered and trembled when they moved, which they did frequently to reach for the large pots of beer at their feet. 'Look at that Billy! All that meat and no potatoes!'

'You're right there,' Billy Bennett said, his stomach rumbling again at the mention of potatoes. 'Hope we don't have to buy 'em by frigging weight. Christ,' he said, looking at the skinny little Liverpudlian, 'you'll have to work hard at it with one of them tarts – the size of them!'

'Get it off,' Ginger said happily, 'they're all the same, big or small, when they're on their backs with the pearly gates open. Come on. We ain't got all day.' He started to push his way down the hall, which stank of cheap tobacco, cheaper scent – and sex. Around them they could hear half a dozen different tongues – German, French, Dutch, Flemish... For the estuary was used not only by ocean-going ships, but by barges from all over Europe, using the great Rhine-Maas link to take their cargoes to Rotterdam and Antwerp for shipping overseas.

A big man in a reefer jacket with a water glass of *Genever* in his hand barred their progress – to Ginger it seemed almost deliberately. 'Let the dog see the cat, mate,' the Liverpudlian said with a winning smile on his skinny face.

The man, dark face sinister and menacing, looked down at Ginger. 'I don't like English,' he announced.

'Can't do nothing about that, mate,' Ginger said, cheerfully enough, his mind on more urgent things.

The man held a hand like a small steam shovel to his nose. 'English – they stink,' he said. Around him his cronies, all big men like himself in reefer coats, with black, peaked caps pushed to the backs of their heads, guffawed hoarsely.

Billy Bennett's face darkened. 'You mind yer words, mister,' he said through suddenly gritted teeth, 'or I'll be giving yer the old whatfor.'

'Whatfor? What is this?' the man in the reefer asked.

Ginger gave Bennett a shove, 'Come on, Billy. Let's get to them pearly gates. No time for arguments now. He's probably pissed anyway.'

Billy let himself be persuaded. Behind him the man in the reefer sneered, 'Typical English – they no like to fight. They run away, *hein.*' Again his cronies laughed.

Ginger pretended not to hear. Instead he crooked his finger at a blonde (though he could tell that she wasn't a natural blonde). 'What about you and me having a nice time, ducks?' he said.

She nodded. She took a deep swig of her beer and rose ponderously. 'What you want, sailorman – once round the world, eh?' Her English was badly accented, but she knew the professional terms all right, Ginger told himself happily.

'No, luv. Haven't got the time. Just a straight job. Get the dirty water off me chest.' He slapped her huge rump joyfully and the flesh trembled and quivered beneath the thin material. 'Lovely grub,' he cried in delight. 'Come on. Let's get up them dancers.' He caught her big hand and started dragging her up the stairs to the bedrooms hastily.

'Hey, you sailorman,' she protested mildly, 'you bin at sea a long time. You such hurry.'

'It seems like a million years. Now come on, move it. I want to show you the big present I've got for yer in me slacks.'

She shrugged and let herself be persuaded.

Moments later Billy Bennett followed with another whore, who was almost as big as he was. Patting his ample stomach, she chortled, 'You fine big fellow.' Then she patted her own large belly and added, 'Not difficult though. I ride you like a horse.' On another occasion and if his need hadn't been so great, Billy Bennett would have blanched at the prospect of being mounted by a whore of that size. Now, all he could comment was, 'Let's hope I win the race, then.'

So it was that the two old shipmates did not see the man with *'De Telegraaf'* come through the open door into the brothel and crook his finger at the man who thought the English were cowards...

FOUR

At first light they got underway. The men were lazy, but happy. All had stories to tell of their amorous episodes and were full of their conquests in that easy manner of young men who have had sexual satisfaction – all except CPO Ferguson.

He had welcomed the afternoon watch with, 'Ay, well ye may look like a lot of lovesick bulls. Ye've had yer pleasure and na doubt the lot of ye'll be poxed up soon. But I'm na having pox and shanker on my boat.' Whereupon he had ordered them to the bow where he had set up his own 'pro station', as he called it: a zinc trough, with three rubber tubes connected to bottles of a purple-coloured liquid, which was potassium permanganate. This he ordered the crestfallen sailors to squeeze – by means of the tubes – into their organs. 'It's the only sure way,' he maintained. 'It'll sting a wee bit, but ye'll na get the pox.'

So, to the embarrassment of the watch, and the bewilderment of the stolid Dutch onlookers, still puffing at those whiteclay pipes of theirs, they were forced to bare their private parts and carry out 'the treatment' as Ferguson called it.

As the *Swordfish* threaded its way carefully and slowly into the river, still packed with barges and coastal freighters heading downstream to the sea, Smith said, 'I aim to get to Arnhem by dark. We'll wait up there till midnight and then have a crack at crossing the German frontier. There'll be no moon and no stars. If we're lucky we can find a barge going the same way and hide on her lee side – something like that. We'll work it all out, when we get there.'

Dickie Bird yawned lazily, his mind only half listening. He had had what he would have called a 'perfectly spiffing' afternoon. He had struck up a conversation with a very pretty girl in one of the many tearooms almost immediately. At first he was a bit worried because the girl – Antje – was too refined and polite. As he had often expounded to his shipmate Smith, 'Sailors don't have time for respectable women, Smith. They've got to be ladies of the night, where goods are exchanged for hard cash. Fact of life.'

Antje, it turned out, had not been so respectable after all. Halfway through her second demitasse of weak China tea, accompanied by petit fours, he had felt a delightful little squeeze on his left knee. He looked down under the fine lace tablecloth to find her small, begloved hand working its way up his trouser leg until it came to the most sensitive spot of his anatomy.

'Thereupon old bean,' Dickie had explained, smiling fondly at the memory, 'negotiations were underway. I feel a chap who rabbits on about filthy lucre in such situations is something of a cad. At all events, coins of the realm changed hands and we popped off to a delightful flat. There in her boudoir, we played the two-backed beast for an hour or so. Quite exhausted – yours truly. However, she said she enjoyed it.' He looked down modestly at his well-manicured nails. 'But no more. A chap should never kiss and tell, what.'

'Exactly,' Smith had agreed with a smile. 'And you'd be the last chap to tell.'

Now with Dickie Bird, still half in a reverie of the delightful events of the afternoon, the *Swordfish* entered mid-stream of the great river, proceeding at a slow speed while the off-duty watch lolled in their civilian finery in the new deck chairs which Smith had bought in Dordrecht, something which had caused CPO Ferguson to have almost a fit. *'Deck-chairs!'* he had exploded when he had found out what Smith's new purchase had been. 'Thirty years in the Royal Navy and we now sail with deck-chairs! I've never heard anything like it in all my born days!' And with that he had marched off muttering angrily to himself.

Now, however, the off-duty men sprawled in the brightly striped chairs, smoking their pipes, waving at little children playing along the banks, whistling at the girls riding along the towpath, their starched white petticoats flying to reveal the usual ample Dutch female legs, and generally acting, as Smith had hoped they would, like wealthy Englishmen out on a continental spree. As Ferguson observed grimly to himself, as he watched their antics, 'Yon folk'll be wanting bluidy tiffin served on a silver tray. Och, my poor *Swordfish,* I never minded we'd sink this bluidy low.'

But while Ferguson raged, the crew enjoyed themselves. Smith, on the bridge, worried. Moving up and down the river, he was able to spot more and more barges and other, smaller craft carrying the flag of the German Republic. While he knew that most of the craft would be legitimate, going about their business of transporting goods and wares to and from the Belgian and Dutch ports, some might not be. He remembered when barges were used, during the war, by both sides to convey spies and agents via neutral Holland to the fighting front in Belgium. He wouldn't put it past the Germans to have some of those seemingly innocent bargees working for their intelligence, reporting back to their headquarters anything suspicious which caught their attention.

He hoped that their roundabout approach to the waterway network and the altered appearance of the *Swordfish,* transformed from a motor torpedo-boat to a pleasure craft, might have fooled this von Horn chap and his agents, but he couldn't be one hundred per cent certain.

By late afternoon, with the sun sparkling off the water and with even Holland's flat countryside looking charming, Smith started to relax; his worries faded. Indeed, he felt almost as if he *were* on a pleasure cruise. More than once, he picked up his binoculars to stare at one of the many windmills of the area or some old church steeple, as if he were really a bonafide tourist, interested in the locality.

Now, as the sun started to sink over the horizon, the barges started to drift to the banks on either side, lying to at the many little riverside inns and fishing hotels. Here, they would gather to eat and drink their *Genever* over cards, slapping the table hard every time they won before turning in for the night.

But, as there was still no sign of Arnhem on the left bank of the great river, Smith ordered that the *Swordfish* would continue to sail until the Dutch city was sighted. From there to Emmerich was a matter of twenty or so kilometres. At two in the morning they would set off, making maximum speed until shortly before the Dutch frontier met with the German frontier. There the motors would be turned off and the *Swordfish* would drift silently – hopefully – past the German custom and immigration posts. Once safely within the country, they would pick up speed. With a bit of luck they would reach the industrial Ruhr, an area now taken over by the French and Belgian occupation powers because the beaten Germans had slackened off their reparation payments to those countries, by dawn. From there their passage would be without danger until they reached Cologne a few hours later.

At the same time, as Smith ordered the *Swordfish* to continue its passage down the darkening river, he also commanded that the deck lookouts should be doubled. As he told CPO Ferguson, 'Chiefie, I'm taking no chances. I know the chaps need their rest.'

'Rest!' Ferguson snorted grumpily. 'Yon layabouts in them fancy trews o' theirn have done nothing else but rest all the bluidy day.'

By six, the river was almost deserted. A few barges were chug-chugging from the direction of Germany, very low in the water, towing behind them other unmanned barges, their bow waves almost level with their stacked decks. 'Reparations from the

Ruhr,' Dickie Bird commented, lowering his glasses, 'they're flying the French flag. Those Froggies are certainly playing merry hell with the Huns.'

Smith grunted non-committally and stared to their rear. Behind them the river was almost deserted save for one lone barge which had been behind them for over an hour now. Its riding lights were on and he could just make a faint glimmer of yellow light on the bridge, but otherwise there was no sign of life on board. He shrugged. Perhaps the crew were down below eating their supper; it was about that time.

Time passed leadenly. Now, slowly, they could see the lights of Arnhem looming up out of the darkness to the left and to their immediate front the huge iron-frame railway bridge which spanned the river at that point. But, if they could spot the street lights, they could see little movements. There were a few cars moving across the length of the waterfront and Smith guessed that like most Dutch towns and villages they had encountered so far, Arnhem had already settled down for the night. It was to the good. They'd be fewer prying eyes to see them tying up and with luck none at all to watch them depart in the middle of the night.

Slowly and carefully, CPO Ferguson, at the wheel, manoeuvred the *Swordfish* into a berth. The engines stopped and the *Swordfish* came to a rest. The crew were dismissed, save for the lookouts, to eat and snatch a few hours' sleep before they attempted to cross the German frontier, while Smith and Dickie Bird retired to the tiny wardroom for pink gins and sandwiches.

Slowly, the fog began to come in, trailing across the great river like a damp grey cat, circling and enshrouding a few craft anchored there, surrounding each boat in a cocoon of its own. Sound was muted. Up river, there was a mournful hoot of a ship's siren as some lone skipper attempted to continue despite the ever-thickening fog.

Smith listened to the faint sound of the siren, as he sipped a tall pink gin and said, 'All to the good, Dickie – the fog, I mean.'

'Navigation'll be harder.'

'We'll take our chance on that.'

'Drifting down the Rhine without power and without navigation lights, old bean.' Dickie shrugged. 'Oh well, the trick is to live well – and make a handsome corpse, what?'

Smith grinned. Good old Dickie, he told himself. Dickie was really a serious sort of a chap, but he always made things seem not quite so serious. What was he always quoting from Oscar Wilde? 'Life is too serious to be taken seriously.' 'Maybe, Dickie. But we're not going to make any handsome corpses this trip, if I have the way of it–' He stopped short. 'I say, what's that?' he exclaimed.

'What's what?'

Smith didn't answer. He craned his head to one side and listened intently. Then he said, with a note of urgency in his voice, 'Listen to that. Whoever he is, he's getting damned close in this peasouper.'

Dickie listened, too, and snapped, 'I say, Smithie, you're right.' He could hear the throbbing noise of a ship's engine quite clearly now and it was very close at hand. 'Is the chappie lost – or drunk?'

'I don't know. But he's getting too close for comfort. Come on, Dickie, let's go and have a look-see.'

They tumbled out of the wardroom, their pink gins forgotten now, and hurried onto the damp, dripping deck. The fog was very dense now. Visibility was down to about five to ten yards. They could just about see the river bank to which they were tied up. But if they couldn't see the craft, they could hear it all right.

'Sounds like one of those big Rhenish barges,' Smith said, peering through the grey gloom, attempting to spot the craft's navigation lights. In vain. There were none. Suddenly he was overcome by a series of apprehension. 'Dickie,' he yelled, 'Sound the siren. *Tootsweet!*'

'Rightho.' Dickie doubled away, his usual bantering tone vanished. He, too, realized the seriousness of the situation. The unknown vessel was coming straight at them.

Up on the bridge, Dickie pulled the klaxon cord hastily. The heavy, dripping silence was broken by the shrill wail of the horn. Once, twice, three times, Bird pulled the cord. Nothing happened. The unknown craft still kept on coming, heading on a collision course. It was then, when there was no response to the signal, and the puzzled crew started to pour on deck, that he yelled to CPO Ferguson, 'Chiefie, there's going to be trouble... *Break out the small arms!*'

FIVE

Now they waited tensely. Each man was armed and ready, all thoughts of sleep vanished. Together they peered through the rolling grey fog, desperate to catch the first glimpse of the approaching vessel before it was too late. For they had no power and no room to manoeuvre, tied up as they were at the jetty with their engines both silent.

'There she is,' Ginger cried suddenly, startling them all. *'The bugger's coming right at us!'*

Next to him, Billy Bennett tensed behind the Lewis gun which had been balanced on a stanchion, holding the heavy weapon in place by sheer muscle power. Automatically, he cocked the machine gun and turned it in the direction of the dark shape now looming out of the mist.

'Christ,' Dickie exclaimed, 'it's the same barge that was following us earlier on. I recognize the cut of her jib.'

'But the skipper must be mad!' Smith cried excitedly. 'He must see us *now!*'

'He has. Look there's light in the bridge. This is deliberate. He's going to crash into us.'

Smith didn't hesitate, though the thought of all the resulting diplomatic complications which might result from his action did flash through his mind. 'Give her a burst across the bows. That might stop the silly devil.'

'Ay ay, sir,' Billy Bennett sang out happily and slammed the heavy wooden butt into his big shoulder. He ripped back the trigger. White tracer spurted from the ugly snout of the Lewis gun. It sailed rapidly across the front of the huge bulk of the barge, while up on the bridge Dickie tugged yet again at the klaxon siren.

Nothing happened. The barge came on. Now it was only a matter of yards away. In a moment it would smash into the wooden sides of the *Swordfish* and that would be that. Smith knew he had to do something – and do it fast. 'Chiefie,' he yelled above the clatter of the machine gun and the steady thud-thud of the barge's engines, 'Start up!'

'But we're–' Ferguson broke off in mid-protest. He pressed the starter button. Nothing. A mere dull click. The barge was almost upon them now. The sweat pouring down his craggy face despite the cold, Ferguson pressed the starter again. The engines fired. He could have yelled with joy. The barge seemed to fill the whole sky now. He slammed both throttles forward. He was going to need full power if he was going to get the *Swordfish* away from the quay and break the stout hawser which tied the craft to it. The boat surged forward. At the stern the twin propellers thrashed the water a wild white. Still the hawser held. At the controls, Ferguson willed the *Swordfish* to break loose, the veins standing out at his temples with the strain. Down below, Billy Bennett was rattling off a whole pan of ammunition at the barge. The tense, expectant crew could see the tracer bouncing off the barge's steel sides like glowing golf balls. Still she came on. They were almost finished now. Smith prepared to shout 'abandon ship'.

Suddenly, startling, the hawser broke. A great singing length of thick rope came whipping across the superstructure taking all with it, as the *Swordfish* streaked forward – and out of harm's way. On the barge there was an immediate reaction. A searchlight flicked on. An icy white finger of light parted the fog. Desperately the man at the tiller tried to swing his clumsy craft round, as the *Swordfish* shot forward, thrashing the water to a crazy fury at its stern. To no avail. Next moment the barge crunched into the side of the jetty. Concrete crumbled. There was the ear-splitting sound of rending metal. A second later the barge came to an abrupt halt.

On board the *Swordfish*, the crew cheered wildly, as the boat surged forward, leaving the crippled, stranded barge to disappear into the fog. 'Cor ferk a duck,' Ginger cried to no one in particular, 'the old Swordie does it again.' Then, looking up at Ferguson's strained, relieved face in the light of the bridge, he called up, 'What about splicing the bleeding mainbrace, Nelson. I think the lads need it after that little carry on.'

Surprisingly enough, Ferguson agreed and now the crew stood about the wet dripping deck, as the *Swordfish* plodded steadily down the Rhine, coming ever closer to the German frontier, drinking strong rum and chatting about the strange episode, until a solemn Bennett, his fat face puzzled, said to Smith, 'Sir, I recognized the chap on the bridge of that barge. Caught a glimpse in the light of that last burst of tracer.'

'You did, Billy?'

'Yessir, me and Ginger over there was in the knocking shop, excuse me, sir, house of ill-repute.'

At Smith's side a relieved Dickie laughed at the big fat man's choice of phrase and said, 'My God, Billy, you'll drink your char with your little pinkie stuck at an angle next.'

'Didn't think it proper to use them words in front of an officer, sir,' Billy Bennett said. 'But anyhow, we was in there when we had a little bull-and-cow with a civvie. Said we

English've got a yellow streak. I was going to paste him one, but Ginger there said–'

'–Get on with it, Billy,' Smith said urgently.

'Well, sir, the feller in the knocking shop was the same feller who was on the bridge of that barge.'

'Oh, I say, that's torn it!' Dickie gasped.

Smith scratched his bare head a little ruefully. 'I dare say it has. It means the swine are on to us again. They've been following us all along ever since Dordrecht. The question is – will they be waiting for us at the frontier?'

Dickie Bird thought for a moment, then raising his voice, asked, 'Did any of you lads see a radio aerial anything like that on that damned barge?'

There was a chorus of no's and a lot of shaking heads.

Smith asked, 'Why did you ask that question, Dickie?'

'Well, that barge captain might have done us a favour. If we assume that he was going to send us to the bottom before we ever reached the Fatherland, then the Huns won't be expecting us to arrive in their country. Now, I hope, the bargee won't be able to report that he has failed in his attempt.'

Smith's face lit up. 'By God, you might just be right, old bean. If he can't communicate and the Huns assume the dirty deed has been carried out, then with a bit of luck we might just slip by the frontier without any further trouble.'

Dickie flashed a look at the glowing dial of his wrist-watch. 'Well, Smithie, in about an hour we'll find out. Now I suggest we go back to the wardroom and resume those pink gins. I feel I need one.'

It was well past midnight. Creeping forward at a snail's pace in the thick fog, Smith tensed as he prepared to open the throttles wide. It was going to be a terrible risk with visibility down to zero, but it was the only way he could give the *Swordfish* sufficient momentum to allow her to drift by the German frontier with her engines not working. Next to him, CPO Ferguson tensed, too. He realized only too well the chances the skipper would have to take in a moment.

'It looks as if we've got about five miles to the German frontier crossing sir,' he broke the heavy brooding silence. 'I ken it's risky, but I doubt if there's a thing out there. I've been harking these last ten minutes.'

'All right, Chiefie, we'll do it,' Smith said through gritted teeth. He started to pull back the two throttles. The *Swordfish* started to pick up speed. The two men could feel the deck begin to vibrate under their feet. Swiftly, her prow rose out of the water.

Smith flashed a glance at the dials. She'd almost reached twenty knots an hour. They were surging through the fog at a tremendously risky speed. God, he prayed there'd be no craft in their way; there'd be one hell of a crash.

To himself, Smith beads of perspiration standing out on his forehead with strain and worry, counted off the minutes. His gaze flashed from left to right, trying to penetrate the grey wall of fog, alert for the first sign of another boat. Then, he'd done it. He pulled back the throttles and turned off the motors. A sudden silence. The hiss as the *Swordfish* slowing down a little, was carried forward by its own momentum. Leaning out of the bridge, CPO Ferguson hissed to the two lookouts on both sides of the bow, 'Keep a weather eye open now, mind ye!'

They didn't reply. They were too intent on their task, peering through the gloom for the first sign of danger.

The *Swordfish* was slowing down noticeably now. Smith told himself they should be at the German frontier, but it was hard to say. They were hemmed in on all sides by that grey gloom. Suddenly he started. There was no mistaking it – the soft put-put of a small boat. There was someone out there. He looked at Ferguson. The old Scot's face clearly registered his shock. Was it the German's authorities? As the *Swordfish* slowed down even more, the steady throbbing of the unknown boat's engine came ever closer.

'Ferguson, take over,' Smith hissed, as if he might be overhead, 'I'm going to have a look-see.' Hurriedly, he clambered down the wet dripping iron ladder that led to the deck.

'To port,' Ginger whispered. He cocked his head to one side, his black oilskin slick and dripping with the wet fog. 'There, sir. Can you hear it?'

Smith nodded and strained too. The boat could be only a matter of yards away. It seemed to be steering a parallel course to the silent *Swordfish,* which by now was moving at perhaps three or four knots. Fortunately, the current was in her favour, helping to carry her along. Smith prayed fervently that it would continue to do so. If the *Swordfish* stopped now – he didn't dare think that thought to its ultimate conclusion.

A harsh voice called something. A moment later a light flashed on. Its beam was broken and refracted by the dense fog. But it was only six or seven yards away. Smith held his breath.

'Wer da?' came the challenge. Smith recognized it for what it was. Had they been spotted?

The sound of the small engine came

closer. The dimmed bean of the spotlight tried to penetrate the fog once again. Smith felt the cold beads of sweat trickle down the small of his back. In his left temple, a vein started to tick nervously. God, he told himself, it could be only a matter of seconds now before they were discovered.

A harsh voice said something in German. Another, much brighter, light flashed on.

'Christ,' Ginger groaned under his breath, 'that's frigging well torn it!'

'Shut up!' Smith hissed urgently.

The light seemed to take an age, as it swung round very slowly, its beam breaking up into a white blaze by the fog. But Smith knew that the unknown craft had come only a couple of yards closer and the spotlight would penetrate the fog and pinpoint them. He clenched his fist impotently, wincing as his nails dug into his palms. If only they could knock the damned thing out!

There was a murmur of voices, as aboard the drifting *Swordfish* everyone froze, all knowing that the slightest sound would give them away now; and knowing too, after what had happened so far, that they wouldn't live to see another day if the German authorities took them. They would be quietly disposed of somehow or other.

A sudden command. The spotlights flicked off. The unknown motorboat started to pick up speed. The sound of its engines began to diminish. The Germans had given up.

Smith breathed out a sigh of heartfelt relief. 'That was close,' he said.

'I tink, I nearly pissed mesen,' Ginger said.

'What d'yer mean – *think?*' Billy Bennett at the other side of the bow grunted. 'I *did.*'

They laughed. They had done it.

SIX

It was a beautiful morning. The sun shone brightly. Over the flat meadows on either side of the Rhine, the swallows soared high into the bright blue sky. Even the cows seemed to be affected by the fine weather. Instead of cropping the grass in their usual slow, dogmatic manner, the sound of the *Swordfish's* motors sent them lumbering across the fields, their great swollen udders swinging from side to side like a clock's pendulum.

Most of the crew, even the off-duty men, were on deck, taking in the sights. All of them had fought the Germans for four years during the war. But apart from Bird and Smith, this was their first glimpse of the one-time enemy country.

'Don't look much different to me, Chiefie,' Ginger opined to the old Scot, as they stared at a pretty little half-timbered farm with a thatched roof, outside which an ancient farmer in rusty black was assembling his cows, with much waving of his stick and curses. 'Could be the old country.'

CPO Ferguson looked at him scornfully. 'Only a Sassenach could talk that kind o' blether,' he declared scornfully. 'Yon German's probably killed more Englishmen than he's had hot dinners.'

Standing nearby, Smith grinned. Next to him Dickie Bird said, 'I say, Chiefie, you are really a one hundred per cent fire-eater, aren't you?'

Ferguson swung round on him, 'With all due respect, sir,' he said cuttingly, 'yer average Englishman forgives too easily. That's your trouble. Now a true Scot – he bears a grudge. For a very, very long time.' He drew the words out and thrust out his skinny chest proudly, as if he had made a judgement about Scots and Scotland which was of some value.

'I suppose so, Chiefie.' He focused his glasses. Up ahead, he could see the smoke ascending from factory chimneys. 'That'll be Gelsenkirchen,' he said. 'The start of the Ruhr district.'

'Ay,' Ferguson said grimly. 'That yon place where Krupps and his like made the cannon to batter our Home Fleet in the war. I hope the Froggies knock the whole place down if the Jerries don't cough up the money they owe them. For once the Froggies'll be doing something right, ye ken, sir.'

Smith shook his head in mock wonder. He had never met a man with such powerful and persistent hates as the old Scot. He dropped the glasses to his chest. 'Just to be careful, we'll lower the flag at the stern, Chiefie.'

'Lower the flag?' CPO Ferguson looked shocked. 'Ye canna do that, sir,' he protested.

'Well, feeling against the Allied occupation powers is probably running high at the moment in the Ruhr. We've taken over their factories and declared martial law. I don't want to provoke any of the local citizenry into throwing half-bricks at us, or anything like that. Let's not stick our necks out unnecessarily. Lower the flag.'

Ferguson went off to carry out the order, but reluctantly, muttering something about 'the disgrace … never seen anything like it.'

Smith smiled and forgot the matter. At this speed they'd be tying up in Cologne by the morning, but it had been a long tiring night, with the crew getting little sleep. Should he order the *Swordfish* to heave to so that the watches could get at least four hours sleep each before they sailed on to Cologne? God knows what lay waiting for them there. Perhaps they would need all the sleep they could get in advance?

'What do you think, Dickie,' he asked Bird a few minutes later, as the smoking chimneys came closer and the brown haze started to increase, progressively cutting out the sun.

'Why not,' Dickie said. 'The chaps need a

rest. We can heave to way off the bank, but out of the shipping lane. The cook can rustle up something decent for the chaps. In fact, what about one of us trying to buy some fresh meat instead of that awful bully beef? They say that with inflation the way it is in Germany now, one single pound will buy you anything.' He nudged Smith significantly, leered and twirled an imaginary moustache.

'All right, you don't have to draw me a picture,' Smith said. In the English papers he had read about the tremendous inflation which currently had Germany in its grips. Workers, it appeared, rushed home at midday with a half day's wages, which amounted to millions of marks, in order to buy a single loaf. If they waited till evening the whole day's wages wouldn't buy the same loaf. It was said that you could live like a prince in a four star hotel on a sovereign a day. Germany's currency, in other words, was totally worthless. The only things which counted were those things which could be sold or bartered on the black market – cigarettes, coffee, foodstuffs etc. 'A good idea, Dickie,' he said. 'But I don't want you to stick your neck out. Just take a couple of sovereigns, no more. Better take Ginger and Billy with you, too. And make sure you're armed,' he added. 'You never know with the Huns.'

'Rightie ho,' Dickie said cheerfully. 'As soon as you're ready, we'll set off. Don't be surprised if you see yours truly herding along a couple of cows or something.'

'I won't, Dickie. All right, you tell Ginger and Billy. I think that spot over there looks a likely one for the night. Get cracking.'

Dickie Bird gasped. Next to him, Ginger gasped too, 'Never seen anything like it in all my frigging born days!' At his side, Billy Bennett said, 'Will yer get a butcher's at that, mates.'

The whole length of the quayside street, fringed by warehouses and red-brick factories, was crammed with jostling, shouting, angry civilians, men, women and children. Some pushed little wooden barrows piled high with stacks of bright, brand-new mark notes. Others, fat and prosperous, smoking thick cigars, were holding up their wares, or letting underlings do their business for them, biting on gold rings, eyeing jewels through professional eyepieces, fingering the quality of pre-war fur coats. All was noisy, anger, confusion – and naked greed.

There were whores everywhere, too. Women in short skirts and knee-length boots, fingering their private parts provocatively or sucking their middle fingers suggestively, eyes empty of anything except greed. With them they had young boys, who constantly ran up to more prosperous looking men, offering them the whores' services. When that proved of no interest, they offered themselves.

'That's the black market,' Dickie Bird announced and for once, his usual blasé manner had vanished. It was all too obvious that this was the real Germany: Germany in defeat, where nothing had any value, but where everything including honour, had its price. The tall, skinny man with the dark glasses and the spotted armband of the war-blinded, who was trying to sell his medals, made that all too clear. 'God, I wouldn't wish this on anyone, even the Huns,' he added grimly.

Billy Bennett nodded and said, 'Over yonder, sir. There's a bloke selling sausages and things.'

'I see him,' Dickie answered. 'Let's go over and see what he's got to offer.'

With difficulty, they pushed their way through the noisy gesticulating throng, dodging the whores and the young touts, thrusting aside a runt of a man who was selling pornographic photos of two stout, Eton-cropped women, until they came level with the man who was selling sausages. He was a great brute of a fellow, in boots and breeches, whose girth suggested he consumed a goodly number of his own sausages. *'Landmettwurst... Grutzwurst... Weisswurst ...*

direkt vom Bauer...'

Dickie Bird nodded his understanding, 'The chap is a farmer selling his own stuff,' he translated for the benefit of the other two.

'Ay, he would be,' Ginger said. 'He ain't been starving hissen – yer can see that all right.'

The farmer-salesman eyed them shiftily when he heard the English. 'Englishmen?' he queried.

Dickie nodded. Hastily he brought out a sovereign. *'Gold,'* he said winningly.

The farmer's eyes lit up. He reached out a pudgy paw for the coin, took it and bit it hard. That satisfied him. 'Good,' he said. 'Here,' he pointed to two large rings of *Mettwurst*. 'You have.'

Dickie looked at Billy Bennett, whose large stomach was already rumbling with anticipation. He grabbed the rings of greasy sausages and slung them over his upper arm like hoops.

'We've got another four sovereigns left,' Ginger remained Dickie. 'We could see what else we could scrounge.'

'Good idea, Ginger. Let's see what we can find for the chaps,' Dickie agreed. 'Let's have a look at that fellow over there. He's got what looks like a fish tank tied to his belly–'

Dickie stopped short. There was a blare of

trumpets coming from the next street and the rattle of kettledrums beaten at a fast pace, accompanied by the swift, crisp crunch of marching feet.

'Die Franzmanner,' the cry went up from the crowd. *'Die verdamnten Franzosen!'*

In an instant all was turmoil. Cases and trays were hurriedly repacked. Currency dealers thrust wads of foreign notes into their hiding places. A fat policeman, who had been watching the dealers with a well-meaning smile on his face, swiftly pocketed his last bribe and disappeared down a side-street.

Then they were there. Great black Senegalese with their faces covered in ritual tribal scars. At their head, on a white charger, a little poppin-jay of an elegant officer, white kepi tilted at a rakish angle, silk cloak thrown carelessly over his thin shoulders, rode.

'It's the Froggies,' Billy Bennett exclaimed as the Senegalese marched straight into the throng, undeterred by the whistles, boos and threats of the mob. Cases went flying. Eggs were trampled underfoot. An enraged German tried to pull the little officer from his mount. All he got for his efforts was a slash across the face from the officer's riding crop. He reeled back as the Senegalese started to lam into the crowd with the brass butts of their rifles.

'Hang on to those sausages, Billy,' Dickie said hastily. 'I think discretion is the better than valour on this occasion. Let's do a bunk.'

The other two needed no urging. Already a couple of shots had been fired, whether by the troops or by the civilians they didn't know or care. A civilian was already writhing in the gutter, blood jetting in a scarlet arc from a wound in his chest.

Now they started retreating down the street, as up above windows were flung open and civilians started raining down missiles on the Senegalese and their officer. He raised himself in the saddle, tugging out his revolver. He fired once. There was a scream. A man sagged wounded – or dying – over a window sill.

A primitive scream of mass fury went up from the crowd. A half a hundred men thrust forward at the French colonial troops. The officer's horse reared up whinnying with terror, as someone slashed at its hocks with a cut-throat razor. The officer fell, disappearing beneath the feet of the mob. Then, the three shipmates were round the bend, out of sight, to be confronted by a lorryload of German police in their black leather helmets, smoking and chatting calmly with one another, as if all was right with the world…

'It's the law of the jungle out there, Smithie,' Dickie said, toying with the sausage, his appetite vanished now after what he had just seen. 'The crowd took one of the blacks they had captured down the side-street and hanged him from the nearest lamppost and the bobbies just watched. Didn't lift a finger. God, that anything like that should happen in the Old Country!' He shuddered violently and had a quick drink at his pink gin. 'As for the officer – they simply trampled him to death. Could hardly recognize him. Just a red smear on the pavement. Poor chap.'

Smith nodded and looked out of the porthole. Fires were burning in the industrial city now all along the waterfront and faintly, he could hear the muted sound of rifle fire. A French plane was swooping low over Gelsenkirchen and a French police launch was skimming down the centre of the Rhine, going at top speed. It appeared the French occupation powers had yet another riot on their hands.

'What you have just said, Dickie,' Smith said, his face unusually serious, 'makes me even more determined to see this thing through. I don't know the rights and wrongs of the French case, but it is clear that law and order is breaking down in Germany. And you know what they used to say – when Germany sneezes, the rest of Europe catches a cold. We've been through one lot of that five years ago. We don't want another dose.'

'Agreed,' Dickie said, still very morose. He was used to the savagery and bloodshed of war. But he was not accustomed to the sheer animal hatred that had come from the mob. There had been something bestial, atavistic about it, as if man had reverted to his primitive state.

'Tomorrow we will be in Cologne,' Smith continued. 'McIntyre will put us in the big picture.' His jaw hardened suddenly, steely blue eyes gleaming with sudden purpose. 'Then, we're going to do our damnedest to stop this feller Hitler before he sets Europe ablaze once more!'

Dickie Bird lost his dazed look. His young face blazed, too, with sudden animation. He said, 'You're right. By God, you're right. *We'll stop him!*'

SEVEN

'The British Army Headquarters is there just behind the cathedral,' Smith announced as the *Swordfish* nosed its way through the traffic under the Hohenzollern Bridge.

Dickie stared up at the soaring Gothic cathedral, which had taken six hundred years to complete, then beyond to the Hotel Dom, overshadowed by the great church. 'Looks impressive,' he said, as they came to a stop and Billy Bennett sprang over the side to tie up the *Swordfish.* Hastily Smith gave his instructions to CPO Ferguson, who was in charge now, and then he and Dickie set off for the hotel HQ.

There were beggars everywhere, many of them cripples from the war. Mostly they were men who had lost an arm or a leg, but there was one unfortunate who had lost all four limbs and who propelled himself along on a little wooden cart with what looked like oars attached to the stumps of his lost limbs.

But there were rich, smartly dressed men and women, fat and prosperous, who sailed through the crowds of importuning beggars as if they simply didn't exist. They were obviously the ones who had profited from the war and had put their money into goods and not into the worthless paper which the *Reichmark* had become.

There were British soldiers aplenty as well. Smartly dressed, swinging their little canes as if they were back on some English barrack square, they strode down the streets. Here and there civilians took off their caps as a sign of respect. But Dickie and Smith could not but help notice the look of hatred in some of the gazes which followed their passing.

They swung round the corner. There was the Dom Hotel, guarded by smart-looking soldiers, their equipment gleaming, their boots immaculate. Important-looking staff officers strode in and out and there was much stamping of boots and saluting.

'If it moves salute it, if it don't, paint it,' Dickie said cheerfully. 'That's the good old British Army for you.'

Smith chuckled too and they continued till they reached the open window of the little wooden guardroom just in front of the hotel's portals. A sergeant with a waxed moustache looked out at them. 'What d'yer want?' he asked, looking them up and down, as if they might just well have crawled out of the woodwork.

'We'd like to see a Major McIntyre,' Smith said.

The sergeant sniffed. The accent was English all right and it was posh. 'All right,' he said, slightly mollified, 'I'll ring his office.'

A couple of minutes later McIntyre was hurrying out of the door personally, as tough and as unsmiling as ever, obviously pleased to see them. 'I've got news,' he said when they were out of earshot of the NCO. 'First, I want to show you somebody. Come on.' Without any further explanation, he bustled them round the back of the hotel to some steps which obviously led to a cellar, in which a tall, immaculate NCO of the Guards stood sentry. When he saw McIntyre he stamped his foot down and saluted.

'All right, Sergeant Hurt ... cut out the bullshit ... I want these gents to see the prisoner. Open up.'

'Yessir ... exactly, sir ... straight away, sir.' Swiftly, Sergeant Hurt pulled a key from his pocket and opened the lock.

Slightly puzzled by it all, Dickie Bird and Smith passed into a gloomy passage and followed McIntyre down a dusty corridor to another door. McIntyre rapped it three times swiftly and snapped, 'It's all right, Dietz. It's me.'

The door was opened to reveal a small man whose face bore the fading marks of what appeared to be a series of large bruises.

Beyond, seated at a table in front of a wireless transmitter, another civilian sat with earphones set on his head.

'This is Dietz, my assistant and interpreter,' McIntyre introduced the little man with the bruised face, 'and that fellah over there, he's our tame Fritz.'

Dietz bowed stiffly from the waist and said, 'Whisky, gentlemen?'

'Sure, why not,' McIntyre said easily, although it was barely ten o'clock in the morning. 'It'll help to entertain you while I tell you my boring story.'

Smith looked at Bird. His look said: 'Nothing boring about what our Colonial is going to tell us, to judge by the situation in this place'.

They sat on packing cases, sipping whisky from chipped enamel mugs in the yellow light cast by the single electric bulb, while McIntyre told them how he had rescued his assistant Dietz, who regarded him now with dog-like devotion, and taken four German prisoners. 'They thought themselves pretty tough hombres, but I managed to persuade them to sing in the end.' He looked down at the knuckles of his right hand, which they could now see were bruised, and the two young shipmates could guess just how McIntyre had made them 'sing'.

'Who were they then?' Dickie asked, unable to restrain his curiosity any longer.

'Members of von Horn's intelligence set-up. All former petty officers in the Imperial Navy during the war. That one,' he indicated the man at the radio, who seemed oblivious of what was going on behind him, 'was sparks on the Hun battleship the *'Derrflinger'* at Jutland. All out of work and down on their luck. So they took up with von Horn and did his dirty work for him – this time, however, one time too often.' He gave that hard, crooked smile of his, obviously pleased with himself.

'It's clear then,' the Canadian continued, 'that von Horn's outfit is working with and for Hitler. It's clear, too, that von Horn is providing the intelligence about the British Army of Occupation, which these nationalists need to prepare their strike.' He nodded to the man at the radio. 'That tame Fritz was their sparks and that's their radio with which he keeps in touch with von Horn's HQ in Flensburg.'

'Keeps?' Smith queried, noting the use of the present tense.

McIntyre's face cracked into another hard smile. 'Yes, you heard right. But the Fritz sends only the stuff we want to be sent. He's working for us now. When the business is over, I've promised him a South American passport, passage to that continent and enough money to tide him over for a while. C's agreed to that.'

'But where are the other three?' Dickie asked in bewilderment.

'Well, they weren't so co-operative. Besides I didn't have the men to keep them under constant guard and I couldn't risk them escaping and blabbing everything to their boss, von Horn. So I sent them abroad – for a little holiday, kind of.'

'Abroad … holiday?' Dickie stuttered.

'Yes, currently the three of them are enjoying the facilities of the Aldershot glasshouse.'

'You mean the British Army's military prison?' Dickie gasped. 'But how did you get away with that? They're not soldiers and they haven't committed a military crime.'

'I know, I know. It's completely illegal. But you know, Bird, if you've got C behind you you can get away with stealing the crown jewels.' His tough grin broadened 'I guess they're going to be three very unhappy Fritzes if any of their fellow prisoners happen to have been in the trenches in the last show. There'll be powdered glass in *their* porridge every morning, I shouldn't be surprised.'

Smith and Bird nodded their heads in agreement, while Dietz beamed at the thought, telling himself the swine deserved everything that was coming to them after what they had done to him in Koeln-Kalk.

'So let me sum up,' the Canadian said,

very businesslike now. 'One, we know this Hitler chap is going to attempt to start a revolution and hopes to overthrow the socialist government in Berlin. Two,' he ticked off the second point on his nicotine-stained fingers. 'Von Horn, representing the traditionalist and right wing, is going to help this Hitler by providing him with the intelligence he needs for his attack on our people here. Three, there is no definite date yet set for this attack. It will come from the north over that radio,' he indicated the German operator in the corner. 'Four, but if we don't know the date, we *do* know the target.'

'And what is it?' the two of them asked in unison.

'Not *what,* but *who!'* the Canadian corrected them.

'All right then who?' Smith snorted a little impatiently.

'General Sir Alexander Godley.'

'And who's he when he's at home?' Dickie asked cheekily.

'Well, for one thing he's a damned fool,' McIntyre said contemptuously. 'Won't listen to anything I have to say, or his own staff officers for that matter.'

'But who is he?'

'The Commander-in-Chief of the British Army of the Rhine, that's who,' McIntyre snapped and there was no mistaking the sudden anger in his voice…

McIntyre had waited, fuming, for nearly a whole day before the great man had finally deigned to see him in the large, requisitioned villa on the banks of the Rhine which was his official home. He had been ushered into the Commanding General's office by a full brigadier and found Sir Alexander in full gear, including spurs and polished riding boots, seated on a saddle instead of a chair behind his desk, which was devoid of one single paper.

He was a tall skinny man, his hair and trim cavalryman's moustache both very white. But he had that peppery look about him of the old school British officer who always aroused McIntyre's ire. Instinctively, he felt his hackles rise as the GOC snapped in a no-nonsense voice, 'Now what's all this rubbish about? My brigadier there,' he indicated the staff officer who was standing rigidly to attention, as if he were still a gentleman-cadet back at Sandhurst, 'tells me the Huns are going to shoot me.' He chortled and his skinny Adam's apple shot up and down his withered throat like an express lift. 'What!'

'That's my information, sir. Can't tell you where I got it. But our own intelligence authorities back in London will confirm it.'

Sir Alexander shot him a hard glance. 'Secret Service, eh?' he barked. 'Lot of nervous nellies. Never trusted them in the last show, what!'

McIntyre ignored the remark. He could see the GOC was a typical hidebound officer of the old school. Instead of arguing, he said, 'Your personal security is not very good sir and we've had plenty of cases of attacks on our people when we never caught the Germans involved.'

'My security is all right, Major,' the General snorted. 'Got a platoon of infantry on duty here twenty-four hours a day. Smart lot of chaps from the West Yorks, what!'

'Yessir. But you do go out riding, for instance, each morning along the Rhine, accompanied only by your groom.'

'I have my riding crop and the groom has his. Hopkins is an old soldier – Fourth Hussar – he knows how to handle himself, what.'

McIntyre felt his temper rising. 'If this old bastard says "what" again, I'll explode,' he told himself.

But there was no need to. Sir Alexander announced with an air of finality, 'Well, I'm an extremely busy man. That will be all.' Before he had realized it, he was being ushered out. As the door closed behind him he heard the GOC chortle, 'Some sort of Colonial, wasn't he? Always a bit jumpy under stress. Were in the last show. Now about that chukka…'

'And that was that,' McIntyre concluded as he ended his description of this encounter with the GOC. 'Just couldn't get through to him. C declined to intervene. He said the British Army will have no truck with what Sir Alexander calls the "Secret Service". Dates back to the last show. So,' he looked hard at Dickie Bird and Smith, 'until we know for certain what the Fritzes are up to, Sir Alexander's safety depends upon you two heroes. And remember,' he held up a finger in warning, 'if you slip up and the Fritzes do manage to bump off the old fool, it'll be a signal to all the hothead Fritz nationalists on this side of the Rhine. The British Army of the Rhine could have a wholescale, full-blooded revolution on its hands...'

EIGHT

Germany was in absolute turmoil. All over the Ruhr, the workers roused by right and left-wing agitators were in open revolt against their French and Belgian occupiers. Daily there were pitched battles being fought in the streets of the grimy, red-bricked industrial towns. Allied soldiers were permanently confined to barracks. Otherwise, they stood a chance of being murdered on the outside. French colonial soldiers refused to obey the order. There were numerous cases of rape, or so the right-wing German newspapers maintained. Daily, new banner headlines proclaimed: *'Black French Beast Takes the Honour of German Maiden'* or *'African Savage Straight From the Jungle Rapes Innocent German Child'*. In Essen, a Black Senegalese was found stripped naked and hanging from his neck. His penis had been sliced off and thrust into his open gaping mouth like a thick black worm.

Inflation went through the roof. Now, those workers who still had a job were paid in billion mark notes. Each week these notes were re-stamped in red by the harassed banks, taking their value up even higher. The price of one egg that terrible summer of discontent would have bought 30,000,000 ten years previously! Workers pulled wooden carts to work to receive their pay, piling them up high with billions of brand-new, but virtually worthless notes. Those earning two billion marks a week could afford only to buy potatoes to feed their families. A story going the rounds was that a woman forgot her shopping basket containing billions of marks. When she returned to claim it again, she found the money stacked neatly on the pavement, but the basket stolen!

Profiteers and foreign speculators flourished. These vultures bought up huge estates, priceless heirlooms, great paintings, for a few hundred pounds or dollars. It was said that a private in the American Army of Occupation in Wiesbaden was living with the beautiful daughter of one of the greatest families in the land because he gave her a dollar a week in order to pay for food for her starving family.

Now farmers profited too. Daily, desperate people from the starving cities trekked onto the land, carrying the last of their family treasures in rucksacks. Pale and wan, they bartered away silver, fine porcelain and the like for a couple of eggs or a handful of potatoes. If they were women, the farmers wanted more – their bodies. It was rumoured that farm animals bedded down now on fine carpets and that rough-and-ready farmhands dined off Dresden china. Nightly, farmers went on patrol round their potato fields armed with rifles and shotguns to ward off potato thieves.

Law and order broke down, even in traditionalist Prussia. Thieves broke into the Prussian hero, Frederick the Great's tomb and stole his orders and medals. Churches were regularly looted of their altar silver and baroque angels for sale abroad to collectors. People were routinely murdered on the streets for their possessions. There were cases of cannibalism. In Dusseldorf, a man was convicted of murdering young boys and girls, dismembering their bodies and turning them into meat pies which were eagerly snapped up by the starving population.

Naturally, the Government and the Jews were blamed for the country's ills. But the foreigners, in particular, the men of the Allied occupation armies, came in for the most blame. They had sucked Germany dry with their demands for reparations; they had seduced German womanhood and made whores of them; and, above all, they had destroyed Germany's dignity and pride in itself.

The Berlin *Deutsche Zeitung*, under a

flame-red headline which demanded, *KILL THE LOT!*, stated, 'Workmen of Germany! It is time you realized the shame the Armistice and quasi-peace has brought on you and your country. Do you still not carry in your hearts that pride which you cast in the mud on the Ninth of November 1918* It will be difficult to abstain from rising under the influence of National Pride. The day will come soon when all your comrades will think: "We ought to thrash those fellows" KILL THEM! THE LAST GREAT JUDGEMENT WILL HOLD YOU BLAMELESS!"'

In Munich, the new leader of the National Socialist Party read the newspapers with an ever-increasing appetite and excitement. In the evenings, in his favourite *Iokal*, the Burgerbraukeller, he would tell his admiring, fawning followers, 'The time has almost come, party comrades. Those contemptuous reds and Yids in Berlin are on the run. These damned Catholics here in Munich have lost the support of the people, save for the old cronies who fill their churches and the populace, left and right, has turned massively against our occupiers, those damned leeches who are living off the backs of honest German working men!' His

*The date of Imperial Germany's surrender to the victorious allies.

dark eyes blazed fanatically and his followers, Captain Goering, Lieutenant Hess and all the rest, nodded their heads in eager agreement. 'Our people,' Hitler continued in that throaty growl of his, 'are under such enormous pressure that we must either act soon – or they will go over to the communists who are promising them the things they want most – bread and work.'

Night after night he hammered home the same simple lesson, as his listeners sat around the bare, scrubbed wooden table, heavy with great litre mugs of Bavarian beer. 'That one single blow must be struck. It will be the signal which will rouse Germany... *Soon!*' And he would look round the circle of their faces with that masterful, man-of-destiny look on his own face and hiss: 'The hour of revolution has almost come...'

Far away at the other end of the country in Cologne, Smith, Bird and the crew of the *Swordfish* knew nothing of Hitler's plans and intentions. But even in Occupied Cologne, under the strict control of the British Army, they could feel the hatred that prevailed everywhere. The children threw stones, civilians attempted to brush soldiers off the pavement, others spat at their feet as they passed, women muttered angry names under their breath. As Dickie commented, 'The jolly old kettle's on the boil, Smithie.

'Spect it won't be long before it boils over altogether, eh.'

But Sir Alexander Godley, the GOC, seemed to sense nothing of this terrible hatred all around. At eight precisely each morning, his charger would be brought round to the front of the big riverside villa by his groom, the bandy-legged Hopkins. The smart sentries, all polished boots and gleaming equipment, would present arms. The General would say, 'Morning, Hopkins, nice morning,' even when it was raining, and then the two of them, armed only with riding crops, would canter down the towpath in full view of potentially hundreds of assassins.

'It's maddening,' McIntyre confessed in frustration to the two young shipmates. 'He sees absolutely no danger whatsoever. He's either the bravest man I know or the most foolish. I tend to think the latter between you, me and the gatepost.'

All the same, McIntyre did what he could. 'We've got to protect the silly old fogey against himself, dammit.' He had a quiet word with the sergeant in charge of the West Yorks guard platoon, a big Yorkshireman from the West Riding called Machen. Sovereigns changed hands and Machen agreed to put up 'voluntary patrols', he emphasized the word with a wink, at night. They would wear plimsolls and carry coshes and instead of walking the beat like the normal sentries, they would hide in dark corners around the big villa and keep their eyes open for intruders. 'Like we did in the trenches in the last show when we expected a Jerry raid,' Machen explained. 'Why give away yer positions in advance – frigging daft.'

McIntyre agreed it was 'frigging daft' and sent him on his way, knowing those ten sovereigns would seem a small fortune to the big NCO.

'But you're going to be the mainstay of the protection plan,' he told Smith and Dickie as the three of them hunched in the tiny wardroom, drinking the usual pink gins. 'You've been on these kinds of shows for years. You know the drill better than anyone.'

'But if we only knew when, where and how,' Smith protested, 'it'd make the job a damnsight more easy.'

'Well, you don't,' McIntyre snapped, obviously just as nervous as they were.

'But surely,' Smith objected, 'you can figure something out by the kind of questions that von Horn poses to that tame Hun wireless operator of yours.'

McIntyre looked thoughtful. 'Yes, I see what you mean,' he conceded after a moment's thought. 'Yes, von Horn has asked for info about the General's daily routine. And we've given him it straight. When the Old Man gets up, when he comes back from the office – that sort of a thing. He even asked if the Old Boy has a "lady friend", as he expressed it.'

Dickie grinned cheekily. 'Would have thought the General was a bit long in the tongue for that sort of thing.'

Now it was McIntyre's turn to give him that crooked grin of his. 'Well, you're wrong, Bird. Regular as clockwork, every Saturday night, when the staff have all gone. Hopkins, that batman of his, takes the car and brings a certain lady of the town to spend an intimate hour with the Old Boy. Regular as clockwork – Saturday night between nine and ten.'

Smith whistled softly. 'The dirty old man! Isn't he married?'

'Widower,' McIntyre replied. 'Anyway, let's get on. Von Horn knows his routine exactly. We gave him the info because we thought von Horn might use it to pinpoint a time when he would strike. So far – no dice.' He shrugged. 'But we're working on it. In the meantime, I want you and your chaps to tighten up security along the Rhine frontage of that damned villa of his. I've tried twice to get him to move to the Hotel Dom, but he won't have it. Perhaps it's on account of the lady of the night.' He sighed like a man who is sorely tried.

'Are you sure they'll come over the Rhine?' Smith asked.

'Pretty sure. I don't think they'd use a local to assassinate his nibs. The way I see it is this. Von Horn and Hitler will try to show that the people on this side of the Rhine are the poor oppressed, kept down by the brutal occupation powers. A true German from the *unoccupied* part of the damned country has taken it upon himself to strike the first blow for freedom by risking his life to come across the Rhine and assassinate the English tyrant.'

'Yes,' Smith said thoughtfully. 'I'll buy that. It would be the kind of dramatic action that this Hitler chap could capitalize on. It would be a very great coup for him and his party if he could claim that it was one of his followers who had done the dirty deed.'

'Exactly,' McIntyre agreed. 'So what can we do in the meantime, until we find out more of von Horn's intentions? I suggest you run a floating patrol the length of the river to a mile of each side of the villa. That should be cover enough. I'll get a wireless set for that big Yorkshireman and you'll keep in contact with him during the time of the patrol to warn him of anything untoward – suspicious. That'll keep him on his toes.'

The other two nodded their agreement. McIntyre reached for his battered cap, stuck it on his hard head at a rakish angle, saying a little wearily, 'Well I guess that's about all we can do for the time being. Be seeing you.' And with that he was gone once more.

The days passed. Now their guard duties had become routine and perhaps a little boring. As CPO Ferguson growled, watching the General and his groom disappearing down the towpath yet once again, 'I dinna join the Royal to act as a wet nurse to some Sassenach general, who's an awfie old fool.'

To which Ginger replied cheekily, 'Now then Chiefie, we all know that before Nelson asked Hardy to give him a last kiss, he asked you for one.' And he blew the red-faced old CPO a wet kiss.

But if they were bored by their task, all of them, even someone as insensitive to what was going on around him as easy-going Billy Bennett, could sense the ever-rising tension. The Germans were getting nervous, touchy and ever bolder. There was a rash of slogans painted on walls in the centre of the old town proclaiming, '*Tommies Go Home*'. A company of young soldiers straight from home disembarking from their troop train at Cologne's *Hauptbahnhof* were booed by a crowd of German travellers. Once, someone tried to pull down the Union Jack which flew in front of Army HQ in broad daylight. It was only when one of the sentries threatened to shoot him that he desisted. At night from over the other side of the Rhine men with loudspeakers shouted patriotic slogans in German, telling their fellow countrymen in occupied Cologne that the time 'of liberation from the English yoke' was not far away. 'Germany for the Germans,' they cried in the darkness. 'Out with foreigners...'

At night now, crouched in the little wardroom before setting off on the nightly patrols, Smith and Bird listened to the taunts, each man wrapped in a cocoon of his own thoughts and apprehensions. They knew it couldn't be long now. The situation had reached the crisis level. If only they could act! This damned waiting was getting on all of their nerves.

But when it came, the news shocked them. It was the big hefty sergeant of the West Yorks who first brought the news to their attention. 'Wanted ... wanted on the blower tootsweet, sir,' he gasped as if he had run all the way from the villa. 'It's that Canadian – Major McIntyre – wants you on the phone at once.'

Smith flashed Dickie a look. Instinctively, the two of them knew that this was the call to arms.

At the double they followed the panting sergeant to the little wooden guardroom outside the main villa. A sentry was holding the phone. Smith took it out of his hand and ordered him and the sergeant outside before he rasped, 'Smith.'

'McIntyre. The balloon's about to go up,' the Canadian said, hard and direct. 'Our tame Fritz had been ordered to alert his comrades to monitor his nib's villa on the Saturday after the next. They are to report everything that happens on that. As soon as *it,'* McIntyre emphasized the word, 'they are to cross the Rhine and report at once. You can guess what "it" is?'

'Yes. The murder of Sir Alexander.'

'Exactly. So now we know,' McIntyre added, his voice suddenly reflective. 'Now it's up to us to outguess the murderous bastards. I'll be in touch.'

The phone went dead. A sudden cold finger of fear traced its way down Smith's spine.

The stage was set, the actors were in place, the drama could begin...

BOOK THREE

END RUN

'Sin, thy name is Woman.'

Old German Saying

ONE

Von Horn sat at his desk, sucking at the end of the inevitable thin black cheroot. Outside, a fat sailor, with his beribboned cap stuck at the back of his head, was lazily pushing a broom down a path in a weak attempt to brush away some leaves, his vest hanging out of his slacks, contrary to Navy regulations. Von Horn sighed faintly. Before the war, a sailor dressed like that and lazing in that kind of manner would have been heading straight for the guardroom before his idle feet could have touched the deck. What a devil of a mess the Fatherland was in in this year of 1923! Those Reds and Jews in Berlin had ruined the country. He sighed again.

Outside, a small group of recruits, heads shaven, totally naked save for their boots and caps, were marching to the swimming pool for their training. He looked at them closely, eyes fixed on their tight white rumps, bouncing delightfully. How beautiful they look, he said to himself, feeling that old familiar stirring in his loins, his heart beating a little faster with lust.

The sight cheered him up. In the new

Germany promised by Hitler, all young men would look like that. Clean and tremendously fit, contemptuous of the soft, effete life of the cities with their degenerate women and the decadent sex practices that always ruined young men. He took a determined puff at his cheroot and pressed the bell on his desk.

Bartels, big, brutal and broken-nosed, appeared at once, as if he had been listening behind the door all the time. '*Herr Kapitanleutnant?*' he rasped, in a voice weakened by years of cheap cigars and even cheaper gin.

'Has the creature arrived?'

Tough as he was, the big petty officer looked a little frightened. '*Jawohl, Herr Kapitanleutnant.* I've put him in the side room–'

–'Did you lock the door?' von Horn asked anxiously.

'*Jawohl.* The fewer people who see him the better, I thought.'

Von Horn didn't believe in petty officers thinking. In this case, he did. He said, 'You did quite right, Bartels. All right, you can show him in. But first get a pistol – and Bartels–'

'Sir?' the petty officer paused at the door.

'Stay with me all the time he's present in this office, please.'

'I will sir.'

He went out and swiftly von Horn stubbed

out his cheroot. He opened the drawer to his desk. His service pistol lay there. He cocked it hurriedly, clicked off the safety catch and replaced it, leaving the drawer slightly open for quick access. You never knew with the 'Beast', as he was called in the service. He was totally unpredictable. More than once a very frightened von Horn had seen him dragged away in a strait-jacket and even then it had taken half a dozen burly men to restrain him.

He knew little of the 'Beast's' history. He knew the creature had been badly wounded in the face by a shell at Verdun in '16, where he had won the *'Pour Le Merite'* for bravery. It was on account of the medal that the Kaiser himself had ordered that the hopelessly wounded young lieutenant should receive the best medical treatment available in the Fatherland. For two and a half years Germany's top surgeons had worked on repairing his face. They had given him a new chin and had made an attempt at replacing his non-existent nose. It had been slow, painful work, with the 'Beast', half drugged most of the time, passing in a dream through the flight of the Kaiser, the establishment of the new republic, the various revolutions, while surgeons came and went.

They had first realized that he was mad in 1920. He had asked for a woman that summer. The doctors had considered the request quite seriously in a three hour long conference attended by *La Charite's** most senior medics. Finally, the majority agreed that a woman should be found for him among the city's many whores. She had been selected with care: an elderly whore thought to be unshockable, who, in the past, had 'serviced' other patients who had suffered mutilation during the war. But it hadn't worked. The whore had backed off, crying, 'No, I can't do it! Even if you paid me all the gold in the world.'

He had followed her from the little room they had provided for the encounter, completely naked and still erect, hissing in that strange reconstructed voice of his, 'I want a mirror… Get me a mirror!'

A terrified nurse had run to fetch him one and, for the very first time since he had been wounded four years before, he had seen his face. The impact had been horrific. He rushed to the nearest wall and had begun to beat his head against it. When one of his surgeons had run up and tried to stop him, he had croaked, 'What have you done to me? Oh my God, what have you done?' He had seized the doctor by the throat and had begun to choke the very life out of him. It had been the quick thinking of another

*A famous Berlin hospital.

doctor that had saved the surgeon's life. He had happened to have a hypodermic, filled with a powerful sedative in his pocket. Without hesitation, he had shot the full dose into the 'Beast's' naked rump. He had gone out like a light, but he had been restrained in a strait-jacket for forty-eight hours until he had promised to behave himself.

He had first come to von Horn's attention a year before when there had been a series of horrific murders in the capital: attacks on women, whose faces had been shattered or virtually ripped off with frenzied, almost demoniacal violence.

It had been the 'Beast' of course. One of his doctors had explained the reason, as he saw it, to von Horn. 'He believes women don't like him because of his shattered face. But he also believes it isn't the wound he received at Verdun that caused his terrible disfigurement, it's the women themselves. So he *takes,* I think that's the only word that can describe his action, their faces from them in an act of revenge.' The doctor had sighed and added, 'Naturally, he should be in a home for the criminally insane, but who would have the nerve to do that to a man with his war record and in the light of the terrible suffering he had gone through?'

'Who indeed,' von Horn had echoed, realizing that this was the very man he needed. The 'Beast' had the strength of an ox; he had nothing to lose but his life; and his hatred could be manipulated to make him kill anyone the manipulator wanted.

Von Horn had become that manipulator. First, he had found a woman for the 'Beast': one who could not be shocked by his looks, simply because she could not see them. 'Blind Klara', as the little middle-aged whore had been called in Hamburg's red light district, had thought her number had come up in the Prussian State Lottery when he had offered her a small flat, a fixed income and as much *Korn* as she could drink if she looked kindly on a badly wounded young officer who had been decorated with the country's highest war medal by the Kaiser himself. She had accepted with alacrity, and in this manner, von Horn had managed to tame the 'Beast'. To a certain degree at least.

Then, von Horn had worked on him, turning his terrible rage against women to one directed against those who had betrayed the Fatherland and naturally he, himself, for hadn't he suffered terribly for Germany?

Once that had been achieved, von Horn gave him his first mission: the murder of a leading socialist politician who was beginning to investigate the secret funds which allowed von Horn's illegal intelligence organization to operate. Like all the politicos, the socialist had surrounded himself with bodyguards. That hadn't worried the Beast one bit. He had thrown open the fellow's door, shot one bodyguard in the knee and before the other could draw his revolver, he had blasted another shot into his face. The shattered face had dripped on to his dying chest like molten red wax.

He had taken his time. He had made the fat socialist swine go down on his knees, begging for mercy, wringing his hands together, tears streaming down his ashen face. Then, after he had had his pleasure with the politician, he had placed his pistol at the back of his skull and blown his head off.

Thereafter, there had been at least half a dozen murders. The 'Beast' had drowned a rich Jewish publisher of left-wing books and newspapers in his own bath, holding him under water until he had perished, while down below in his palatial mansion the servants came and went. In a frenzied attack, he had virtually ripped the head off the bolshevik mistress of a high ranking Reichswehr officer who was selling military secrets to the Reds... Whenever von Horn had given him a mission he had carried it out without question, his mood before and after the killings bordering near to madness. It was then that Blind Klara had to use all the tricks of her profession to soothe him down, so that there would be no need to bring in the doctors and their strait-jackets.

Now, as he waited there for the 'Beast', von Horn felt that old sense of foreboding and downright fear. The 'Beast' was too unpredictable. The madness that possessed him and gave him his enormous strength could break through – permanently – at any moment. Then the 'Beast' carried away by his dementia, would kill regardless of purpose or person. He slipped his fingers into the drawer and felt again the reassuring hard gun metal of the pistol. If it ever came to that, he told himself, he would shoot the 'Beast' himself like the mad dog he was.

'Sir,' it was Bartels at the door. 'Your visitor–'

Bartels never finished his introduction. A great hairy paw, the nails chewed to the quick, was thrust in front of him. With one swipe the paw knocked the petty officer to one side.

The 'Beast' lurched drunkenly. He swayed in front of von Horn's desk, while the latter forced a smile, though he had never felt less like smiling; he was too afraid. He stared up at the other man. The man's face was a nightmare. The shell had struck from the side in the centre of the face, taking away his nose most of his jaw and one eye. Now, after years of operation and plastic surgery, the medics had managed to repair the worst of the damage. But that martyred face was still a bright lobster red, contrasting with the pallor of the rest of the skin, cracked and fissured here and there like charred timber, with a roll of flesh that acted as a nose visibly held to the forehead by two silver wires. Once again von Horn realized why that first whore had panicked and had started screaming when she had seen that ruined face. Even a hardened pavement-pounder, he thought, could not have lain close to that hideous monstrosity.

'Won't you please be seated, *Herr Leutnant?'* he addressed the 'Beast' with his old rank.

Clumsily, for he had lost all normal co-ordination, the 'Beast' sat his bulk on the chair, dwarfing it with his size, his great legs spread, his two hairy paws, hanging loosely between them.

'I have a task for you,' von Horn said, willing himself with great effort to look at the 'Beast's' face.

The 'Beast' grunted, but showed no emotion or interest.

'A foreigner – very important foreigner,' von Horn tempted him.

'Frenchman?' the 'Beast' growled, showing some interest at last. 'I've killed French before this–' he pointed one hairy finger at his face. 'Lots of them. Like to kill another one.'

'No, not French, but English – a very important Englishman, in fact. A general ... the commander of an English army.'

The 'Beast's' slack mouth started to drool saliva from the left side. It was almost as if he were a real animal, already savouring the taste of the kill to come. 'A general,' he echoed. 'Hm, a general.'

Von Horn paused. He knew he had to allow the 'Beast' time for the information to sink in. When he was in action, the 'Beast' moved with lightning speed. But otherwise his thought processes were extremely slow. Again he was like a predatory animal harbouring his strength before a kill. Outside all was silent save for the steady pacing of the sentry on the gravel path. Von Horn felt his fear of this horror grow even more. He flashed a glance at the half open door. A white-faced, tense Bartels stood there in the shadows, pistol in his hand. He, too, it was obvious, was scared stiff of the monster squatting in the chair in front of von Horn's desk.

Slowly, the 'Beast' squeezed his glass eye out of its pit. He tossed it up and down in the palm of his hairy paw like a marble. Von Horn had seen him do it before. It was a sign that he was thinking. He swallowed hard, fighting back the bitter bile that threatened to make him retch.

Finally, after what seemed an age, the

'Beast' screwed up his face and pressed the glass eye back into its socket. Von Horn gave a barely-disguised sigh of relief and waited.

'I'll do it,' the 'Beast' said ponderously, as if he had difficulty in stringing too many words together. 'When … where?'

'Next Saturday. Cologne. Now listen…'

TWO

Sir Alexander sat on his saddle-chair, one hand dug deep in the pocket of his riding breeches, the other holding the phone. The little doxy at the other end spoke excellent English and it gave him a great deal of sexual pleasure to talk daily with her like this. He was nearly sixty now and not as virile as he had once been. As a divisional commander during the war, every second night he had bedded a French whore in that splendid four-poster he slept in at his chateau HQ. Now he needed to work up his appetite for his weekly Saturday night encounter.

'I shall wear the black lace drawers and the frilly garters,' she was saying in that delightful naughty accent of hers. 'But you must not be a bad boy and remove them.'

'Why not, my dearest? Oh please let me remove them and look at your splendid little thing.'

'Naughty, naughty,' she chided him. 'Oh, aren't you such a greedy man.' She breathed softly into the phone and he felt a sudden surging in his loins. He pressed his free hand deeper into his pocket. 'However, if you are a little good, I shall allow you to kiss my titties.'

'Oh, would you, my darling girl?' he breathed hoarsely, sweat breaking out on his wrinkled forehead at the thought. 'Could I suck the nipples, too, dearest?'

'Only very little and gently, as if you were my own dear baby.'

'Let me be your baby, *Liebchen.*'

'But babies don't do naughty things like sticking things up ladies, do they?' she admonished him.

'But it is so delightful, sweetie,' the General cooed over the phone. 'I think if you were here now' – he tapped the bulge in his breeches to make sure he was right – 'I would do that naughty thing to you right here and now – over my desk. Now, what do you say to that?'

'Oh, if you continue in this manner,' she said very firmly, 'I shall be forced to take your trousers down on Saturday and give you a good spanking, do you understand me?'

The General swallowed hard. He hadn't had a good smacking for a long time now. 'Do you really mean that?' he asked thickly.

'I certainly do, you naughty boy. Your bottom needs a severe smacking for saying such terrible things to your darling darling little pussy cat–'

Listening in on the extension outside, the

General's groom and batman, Hopkins, shook his head in mock wonder. The old fart, he told himself, will have a heart attack if he goes on like this. The boss was getting too old for that kind of thing. He'd have to start putting bromide in his tea like they did with new recruits to make them concentrate on their training and to stop them having randy thoughts.

Hopkins had a sneaking liking for the 'boss', as he called the GOC. He was toffee-nosed like all the old school cavalry officers of his class, but he was brave and when the division had gone into action during the last war he'd gone with it. Not like so many divisional commanders who spent the war in their *chateaux*, boozing and womanizing. He was worried for the boss, too. He had listened in to the conversation the General had had with the tough Colonial major and the West Yorks NCO had told him how the Colonial had slipped him a few bob to run sneak patrols at night – just in case.

Still the old fart just wouldn't take his security seriously. He frowned. The Jerry tart he rogered on Saturday nights, for instance. She couldn't be trusted either. He didn't trust a single squarehead. She could slip a knife though the boss's skinny ribs one night – and that would be bloody that.

On the other line, the General was quavering in his thin reedy voice, 'Don't torture me any longer, my dearest sugar plum. I know I'm a naughty boy, but you must take them off for me this coming Saturday. I couldn't stand it if you refused an old man's fervent wish–'

Outside, there was the sound of a car braking. The guard commander barked an order. There was the stamp of boots on concrete. Horny palms smacked against rifle butts. It was an officer, Hopkins told himself. He was getting the 'present arms'.

'I shall slip them off your delightful body slowly, very slowly, savouring every precious moment, my darling,' the General was drooling, as Hopkins put the extension down softly and tip-toed the best he could in his heavy, polished boots to the entrance hall, where, seizing a cloth, he pretended to be dusting the hall table.

One moment later, McIntyre came striding in, face like thunder, revolver bulging clearly in the right pocket of his shabby, unpressed uniform. 'Is your master in?' he snapped at the batman.

'Yessir,' Hopkins said, standing rigidly to attention with the cloth held tightly to his side, as if it were a rifle. 'He's on the telephone though, at the moment.'

'Announce me,' McIntyre snapped. 'It's urgent, very urgent.'

'Yessir. I'll see what I can do.'

He tapped on the door and entered softly.

The General perched on his saddle was quite red in the face. It was not surprising. He was on heat. The things she was now saying had made him very excited indeed. The bulge in his breeches was all too pronounced.

'If you dare remove my underthings, I promise you,' she was saying in a very threatening tone, 'that you will have to pay a high price for it, sir. You may have your way with me, have your sordid pleasures, but afterwards, there will be punishment. No sir! Not just with my delicate hand, but with the *whip!*'

The GOC nearly jumped out of the saddle when Hopkins said softly, 'Sir?'

He shook his head like a man trying to wake from a deep sleep. 'I shall call you again, my dear. I've got to attend to something.' He put the phone down hurriedly and, pulling out a large silk khaki handkerchief, wiped the beads of sweat from his red face. 'What is it, Hopkins?' he demanded, feeling that delightful object between his legs receding rapidly through shock.

'It's the Canadian officer, Major McIntyre, sir. He says he would like to see you urgently.'

'Damn the man's impudence,' Sir Alexander snorted, angry at being disturbed in the middle of such a delightful conversation. 'What's up?'

McIntyre was already at the door.

'We know for certain now, sir,' he snapped.

'For certain – *what?*' the GOC snorted, looking at the cold-eyed Canadian in his untidy uniform.

'When they're going to attempt to assassinate you, sir,' McIntyre replied, no trace of emotion in his voice. He might have been speaking of the state of the weather.

'What poppycock!' the General blustered. 'Who would want to shoot me. This isn't Ireland, you know. This is a civilized country – Germany.'

McIntyre didn't allow himself to be rattled, although the man he was speaking to was the most powerful Briton in Occupied Germany. 'It's a political matter, sir. You are a symbol of the enemy occupiers to the boche. Eliminate you and it will be triumph for the German right-wingers attempting to take over power this year.'

'Enemy occupiers, my foot! The Huns seem to like us. The Chief Burgomaster here, what's his name?' He snapped his fingers in irritation. 'Oh, yes Adenauer. He's very friendly and there are other Huns, I know, who like us a lot, a lot better than the Froggies, I can assure you of that.'

With studied patience, McIntyre waited for the General to finish before saying laconically, 'It's this coming Saturday. They plan to kill you on that day, sir.'

The General looked at him, as if he had suddenly gone mad. 'Now how can you know that, man?' he demanded. 'Even if there were anything to all this tall tale, how could you know that so exactly, eh?'

McIntyre stood his ground doggedly. 'I can't reveal my sources, sir,' he said. 'But you can take it that they are absolutely impeccable, sir.'

The General paused. Hopkins, who knew better than most men that the General was getting a bit long in the tooth now, and that of course, that Jerry bint had sent him a bit loopy, knew he was no fool. Even in the British Army you couldn't become a GOC if you were. McIntyre's stand had impressed the old man. He was thinking the Canadian's words over.

Finally the GOC spoke. His temper had vanished. When he spoke now his voice was almost gentle – for him. 'Major, I'm afraid I can't move from this place on Saturday. In the afternoon I've a reception for the colonel of the 8th Irish Hussars and his squadron commanders – they're due out here soon. I can't cancel. Then I have – er – another private matter to be taken care of here that same evening. However, if it will give you any peace of mind – and I can see you take this matter seriously – I'll suggest this.'

'Yessir?' McIntyre prompted eagerly.

'I'll whistle up a company of West Yorks for that day. They can take up positions all around this place. In addition, I'll talk to my friend Dr Adenauer – the Hun Chief Burgomaster chappie – and ask him to supply a *Hundertschaft*. Is that the correct word?'

'Yessir, it is. It means a hundred police recruits from the police training barracks.'

'Well, if I can get them, we'll seal off the whole place.' He gave McIntyre a thin smile. 'In addition, I and my groom here will carry loaded revolvers and I can assure you that we know how to use them. Now then, Major, does that satisfy you?'

'Pretty well, sir. But I have one request.'

'Fire away.'

'Do you think I could take temporary command of the West Yorks company? I was a company commander in the trenches in the last show.'

The General looked at the ribbon of the Military Cross on McIntyre's breast and the three golden wound stripes on his sleeve. 'Yes, I can see you've been through the mill. But why do you want temporary command of that company?'

'They are regulars, sir,' McIntyre said swiftly. 'They're used to the regular way of doing things. But we're not up against regulars. We're up against terrorists. They fight dirty and we've got to be prepared to do the same.'

The GOC nodded his understanding. 'I'll see what I can do. The CO of the West Yorks won't like it, but as it's only for a day, I expect he'll rally around.' He chuckled. 'After all, I am the GOC.'

'Thank you, sir.' McIntyre touched his hand to his battered cap in a vague salute, did an about-turn and went out.

'Well, Hopkins,' the General said sitting back on the saddle-chair, 'what did you make of all that, eh?'

'Bit of a turn up for the books, sir,' Hopkins admitted. 'Funny lot – Colonials. But he looks a hard man to me, sir. I think he knows what he's on about, sir.'

'Yes, I think you're right. All right, then, Hopkins, off you go. I'd better get on with shuffling a bit of this bumpf.'

Hopkins went out smartly and the GOC stared down at the pile of paperwork – approval for promotion, confirmation of court martial sentences, recommendations for good conduct medals, all the mundane letters, orders, forms of a peacetime army – and found he couldn't face it. He put down his fountain pen once more and thought of the Canadian's words. Could some Hun fanatic really be out to do him in? He fought fanatics often in his youth. Fuzzy-wuzzies and whirling dervishes in Africa, Pathans and the like in the Hindu Kush, wogs in Egypt, but he'd always thought of fanatics being natives, black or brown. He'd never considered the Huns as such. He frowned. Since the last show he didn't seem to be able to comprehend the world any more. There were even these labour chappies in Parliament now demanding that the country should get rid of the British Empire!

He let his mind drift. He thought of her in those lace-trimmed black silk drawers she loved to wear. He licked his wrinkled lips in anticipation. 'Damn it all,' he said aloud, 'Terrorists or no terrorists, I'm going to enjoy my Saturday night...'

THREE

'Dusseldorf-Hauptbahnhof Dusseldorf!' The 'Beast' awoke with a start as the great metallic voice echoed and re-echoed in the bare cavern of a main station.

He had been dreaming he had been leading that last fatal charge at Verdun when it had happened. The French machine guns had been chattering furiously, mortar bombs had been exploding all over the place and, here and there in the drifting fog of war on the barren, shell-pitted heights, they had glimpsed the French infantry in their horizon blue. His men were falling on all sides, but they kept on doggedly, braving the hail of steel. Suddenly out of the smoke, Fort Vaux, their objective, had loomed up. 'Follow me, men,' he had yelled, adding the traditional rallying cry, 'the captain's got a hole in his arse!' They had cheered and had begun running again. Then, something had hit him full in the face like a sledgehammer. A sudden spurt of scarlet had exploded in front of his eyes and he had known no more.

The 'Beast' shook his head. He fought off the dream. He tried to remember the instructions von Horn had given him at

Hamburg station when he and Blind Klara had seen him off. He was to go only as far as Dusseldorf. The next station would be Cologne and if he went that far he ran the risk of being checked by the Tommies. If they discovered his two pistols then, as von Horn had put it, using the old front swine's jargon, 'the clock'll really be in the pisspot'.

From Dusseldorf, he was to take the tram to Koeln-Deutz, a suburb in the unoccupied part of the great Rhenish city. Von Horn had said the Tommy crossed every evening after dark to meet the woman. This time when he arrived at his 'love-nest', as von Horn had sneered, 'you will be waiting for him, my dear *Leutnant*. You will do what you have to do, but you must leave clues all the time.'

He had nodded numbly, not quite understanding and not really caring. Every time he was allowed to sleep with Blind Klara he felt a sort of lazy peace with himself – for a while. He was feeling that way now. That terrible rage which animated, burnt within him, had lapsed and the feeling was good.

'You see,' von Horn had lectured him, as they stood there in the shadows waiting for the express to start, 'when the deed is done the Tommies must reveal that the assassin came from unoccupied Germany. It has to be clear that someone – some brave patriotic German – risked his life to rid the Fatherland of the foreign tyrant. That man will become a symbol of German renewal and the German people's bid for freedom. Do you understand?'

Dumbly, he had nodded his head, as the red-capped guard waved his little stick and had shouted, *'Alles einsteigen … alles einsteigen, bitte!'* Klara had hugged him with surprising warmth, for she was not a demonstrative woman, and had cried above the noise of escaping steam, 'Look after yourself, Gerd … look after yourself,' and then, for some reason, tears had begun to flow from those blind eyes of hers.

Now, as everywhere, the doors of the compartments started to slam open, he wondered anew why Blind Klara had cried. Then he dismissed the matter. He took the special key that von Horn had given him and opened the door of his first class compartment. A woman passing caught a glimpse of his ruined face in the yellow light of the gaslamp and shuddered. Hurriedly, he pulled up his coat collar and tugged the brim of his felt hat deeper over his forehead.

Head bent, he pushed and shoved his way through the throng of passengers outside into the glowing darkness. He knew exactly what to do. Von Horn had told him. The tram stop was to the left of the station. He was to catch the one to Koeln-Deutz and sit near the door on the special seat reserved for the 'war mutilated'. There he was to pull down the collar of his coat so that the other passengers would see his face. 'They mustn't forget you,' von Horn had insisted. 'It will be another clue that the press can follow up once the deed has been carried out. It will be quite clear that one of the brave wounded warriors was responsible.'

The 'Beast' had felt quite proud of that description – brave wounded warrior. Still, as he sat there next to a man whose left leg was missing, he detested the covert horrified glances that the other passengers darted at him. Even the man with one leg couldn't bear to look at him, the 'Beast' sensed that. But von Horn had said – it had to be done, so it would be. Yet, now that old rage at what life had done to him started to build slowly. He had been hurt. Soon, somebody else would have to hurt in return.

Half an hour later he was alone in the bare little room of the discreet little *pension* reserved for him by von Horn, waiting for the call to von Horn to come through via the switchboard below in the reception, moodily drinking the glass of *Korn,* which the proprietor had brought him. Somewhere bedsprings were squeaking and someone was giggling softly.

His black mood increased. He was condemned to be out of things for ever. Blind Klara loved him only because she couldn't see him, he knew that. If she could, she'd run away from him. He was certain of that. 'Damnit, what a shitty life,' he grunted and slammed his big paw down on the bed so that the glass of gin on the little bedside table trembled.

The phone shrilled suddenly. He seized the receiver. It was Horn. He wasted no time. 'Have you pencil and paper there?' he rasped.

'Jawohl, Herr Kapitanleutnant–'

'No ranks,' von Horn said smartly. 'You never know who might be listening. Good, this is the woman's address. Schoerner-strasse funf ... Frau Klose. Make sure that you ask the hotel reception for directions. It will be another clue – later. One more thing. The time.'

'Yes?'

'Twenty hundred hours tomorrow night. *Klar?'*

'Klar!' he rasped, as if he were still that bold young Prussian lieutenant of infantry receiving an order to go over the top from his commanding officer.

The phone went dead. Slowly the 'Beast' took the two pistols from his battered brief-case and lay them on the bed. He stared at them, the rage within him beginning to intensify by the instant. Up the corridor, the silly giggling had changed to a harsh strangled gasping. It was almost as if the girl was being choked. The words came slowly from him, formed he knew not how. *'Love … is … death…'*

Nearly four hundred kilometres away in Hamburg, von Horn put down the phone and stared up at the shabby little whore. Her face was still sad and pained and her rouge had run where the tears had trickled down her cheeks. He felt a sense of contempt for her. Women were fools. Unlike men, who could love but keep their emotions under control. Woman always wore their hearts on their sleeves, the silly fools.

'You understand,' he said coldly, 'that when you are approached later, probably by our authorities, there must be no mention of my part in this affair?'

She nodded mutely.

'If you are asked, you will say that he told you he was going to kill an English general as a symbol to the German people. The idea was his own, nobody else's. If you do as I say, you will continue to receive a weekly sum of money, enough to keep you. If you don't…' He left the threat unuttered. He didn't want to frighten the whore into doing something foolish. 'You do understand that?' he said instead.

'Yes, I do.' Her voice was still thick and her mouth quavered, as if she might break down and begin sobbing once more.

'Good. Then you can go,' he dismissed.

She didn't move. Instead she asked, 'If I may ask the officer a question. Won't Gerd be coming back... Would you answer me that, sir?'

He thought quickly, glad that she was blind and couldn't see the look on his face. 'Not for a while,' he said after a moment. 'It's understandable. Your Gerd will have to do a dive until the hue-and-cry dies down. You don't want the police to take him, do you?'

'No sir,' she answered hastily. 'I wouldn't like that to happen to Gerd. He's suffered enough as it is.'

'Yes, he has,' von Horn heard himself say with a note of sympathy, fake as it was, in his voice. Inside his head, a harsh little voice rasped, 'Don't worry, you silly goose, the 'Beast' won't be suffering much longer.' 'All right, are you satisfied now?'

'Yessir. Thank you, sir.' She gave him a little curtsey, as if she were still the little country girl she had once been and not the raddled whore who had lost her eyesight due to syphilis. Without feeling, he watched as she groped her way to the door and walked past the ever-watchful Bartels. He waited till she had gone before he spoke, a note of satisfaction in his voice now. 'Well, Bartels, it looks as if we have done everything we can do.'

'Yessir,' Bartels agreed dutifully. 'As long

as that big madman doesn't go off his head and do something crazy.'

'He won't,' von Horn reassured the other man. 'The 'Beast's' days are numbered. The men in the white coats with the strait-jackets won't be coming for the 'Beast' much longer – thank God. All right,' he was businesslike again. 'Get down to the exchange and tell that fool operator to get me that special number in Munich, you know the one. Tell him it's an "immediate". Oh, and yes, once he's put the call through, watch that he's not got his big ears to the line listening in. The fewer people who know about this, the better.'

'Jawohl, Herr Kapitanleutnant,' Bartels growled and went out, telling himself that von Horn was dealing with that Nazi boss Hitler again, and wondering yet once more why. That braggard was going nowhere.

Five minutes later a hoarse Austrian rasped, 'Wolf!'

Von Horn, the Prussian aristocrat, wrinkled his nose up in distaste. The rabble-rouser's accent was so thick that it was virtually unintelligible, at least to him. And why that ludicrous covername 'Wolf'. The man hadn't one vulpine feature about him. Still, he had orders to work with the man from above. In due course, when he came to power, von Horn's political and financial masters would cut the Austrian upstart down to size. 'Dr Wolf, I have news for you. Operation Five O'Clock Tea is due to start in twenty-four hours' time.'

Hitler chuckled. 'Excellent code-name. Five O'Clock Tea. But this time the English milords will be served a much more lethal brew no doubt?'

'You may be sure of that, Dr Wolf,' von Horn cursed the man inwardly. Hitler had no sense of security. But they'd tame him, knock him into shape, in due course. 'You will act according.'

'I will.'

'Auf Wiederhoren.'

'Servus.' Hitler said and put the phone down.

Von Horn cursed again. Couldn't the man speak German properly?

In Munich, Hitler was not one bit concerned with the class into which he had been born nor the accent with which he spoke. Now, his mind was racing. He knew people like von Horn, those plutocratic northern aristocrats and industrialists, thought they were using him. Let them think that. It would be too late when they found out *he* was using *them*. For the time being, however, he needed them.

He dismissed von Horn and his ilk. He had other, more important matters on his mind. After the killing of the Tommy general, Germany would be in an uproar.

Naturally the English government would put pressure on Berlin to help find the assassin. It was exactly the plot he needed. Those Jews and socialist traitors in Berlin would be seen bowing to the victorious Allies yet once again. They had stabbed Germany in the back in 1918. Now they were doing it again. His dark eyes blazed as he thought of the words he would use. 'The November traitors, German, party comrades, fellow citizens, they are betraying our beloved Fatherland yet once more. It must have an end. This cannot go on. Down with Berlin! Up the revolution!'

He contained himself with difficulty. His chest was heaving violently as if he had actually shrieked the words at the mob. He licked his lips. The death of the Tommy general would be a symbol. Now he needed another. Then he had it. Germany had surrendered to the victorious Allies on November 11th, 1918. Now, five years later, he would set the date of the start of the New Germany – 11th November 1923...

FOUR

Sparks, the *Swordfish's* radio operator, was the boat's youngest and smartest crew member. He was a typical, young, carefree cockney of whom there were many in the Royal Navy. Quick young men, who brilliantined their hair, wore their caps at rakish angles and soaked their number one uniforms so often that they were almost skin tight. All of them had the 'patter', especially when talking to the girls – 'tarts' they called them. When out of the sound of Bow bells, they invariably laced their 'patter' with plenty of rhyming slang, all aimed at impressing the 'tarts' and getting them up the 'apples and pears' as soon as possible.

Often CPO Ferguson would snort in irritation. 'Sparks willye no cut youn blether and speak the King's English like I do?' To which Sparks would reply in his cheeky carefree way, 'Go on, Chiefie! Blimey, you ain't spoke King's English in all yer bleeding life!'

But Sparks had always been noted for taking risks, not only with irate chief petty officers, but also with women. It was not just the many single 'tarts' he had succeeded in getting in 'the family way', it was those married women with jealous, suspicious husbands. Indeed, it gave the young cockney actual pleasure to outwit some suspicious husband and have his 'wicked way'. He would boast to his shipmates of his latest conquest. 'Gor luck a duck, I had her on the sofa in the kitchen while the silly dipstick was digging up the front garden. Should look after his trouble-and-strife better, that's what I say.' And he would go off whistling merrily, as if he hadn't a care in the world, which he hadn't.

Now, this early Friday night, Sparks was going to embark on another amorous adventure, though this time the danger didn't stem from a jealous husband, but from CPO Ferguson. He had spotted Elisa at the beginning of the week when she had been hanging out the washing in her back garden which ran to the back of the Rhine. Stretching up to reach the taut line, her splendid figure and good stout legs had been clearly exhibited against the thin material of her frock. Naturally, she had seen him watching her as he had lounged at the rail of the *Swordfish*. Spontaneously, she had stopped hanging up her 'smalls', as Sparks called them, and waved. That had done it. 'Like giving strawberries to a frigging elephant,' he had said to himself, mind made up. Even if old Chiefie did put him on the 'rattle' for it, he wasn't going to miss a chance as good as that. That night, and on the off-duty watch, he had stolen the little rubber dinghy which the *Swordfish* towed, rowed across the darkening Rhine, and had given the delightful Elisa the 'patter', though his German was limited to *'Ich liebe Dich...'* and *'wo ist dein Bett?'* He had her twice on the kitchen table and was back on the Occupied bank of the Rhine within two hours.

Now it was Friday night and on Friday night as a kid he'd always gone on the 'razzle'. Half a pint of 'pig's ear' at the local boozer. Then, fortified with just enough beer but not too much to give a 'bloke' 'brewer's droop', he'd sally forth to find the 'tarts'.

Tonight, washed, shaved, talcum powder under his armpits and in his crotch, hair sleeked down with cream smelling strongly of violets, dressed in the new duds the skipper had bought them, he manoeuvred the little dinghy into the river, not using the oars, in order to prevent discovery until the craft reached the current. A little bit of hard rowing and some careful steering and he'd land right up close to her back garden. He looked back at the stark silhouette of the *Swordfish,* outlined by the lights of Cologne, and whispered, 'Ta ta Chiefie. Don't wait up for me...'

Frau Klose was terrified of him, the 'Beast' could see that. When he had entered the little riverside cottage, her hand had flown to her mouth, as if she had been about to shriek at the sight of that terrible face. Later, when she had brought him coffee and a roll with *leberwurst,* she had kept her gaze averted as if she couldn't bear to look at him. The knowledge heightened his black rage and he felt he could have slaughtered her there and then, as he had done with those other women in Berlin, but von Horn had expressly ordered him not to touch the woman. 'Frau Klose is part of the tale, *Leutnant,*' he had explained slowly and carefully, as if he were talking to an idiot. 'She is a war widow – husband killed at the front in Italy in '17. Now, this beast of a Tommy has raped her. You know of this because you were a comrade of her husband at Verdun. She has confessed all to you. This is the last straw. You decide that her shame and all the insults heaped on us Germans by those foreign pigs must be avenged. That's the story.'

So he sat there moodily under the single yellow bulb, waiting for the Tommy to come, while she pretended to busy herself in the kitchen next door, rattling the fire irons, doing all sorts of purposeless tasks, no doubt in order that she hadn't to sit with him and look at his ruined face.

He knew what he had to do. He had to kill the Tommy tonight, drag the body to the bottom of Frau Klose's garden, conceal it but not too well. Then he'd take the man's boat, cross the Rhine and abandon it on the other side. On Saturday morning, he would be in position. In the meantime Frau Klose would wait till the morning of Sunday before going to the police to report that she had been raped by the unknown Tommy. The day before, she will have told an old friend of her husband's and he will have gone off in a mad rage to find the Tommy rapist. 'That will start the ball rolling. Neither the Tommies nor the German authorities, those weak swine in Berlin, will be able to hush up the matter, *Leutnant*,' von Horn had sneered.

'Sir,' Frau Klose's urgent whisper broke into his black reverie. 'I can hear him ... his boat.'

For a big clumsy man, the 'Beast' acted with surprising speed. He hurried into the kitchen. Carefully, he peered into the darkness, with the lights of Cologne stretched along the bank on the other side. He made out the dark figure rowing a little boat closer to this side. 'It's him?'

She nodded, not daring to look at him. 'All right, you know what you've got to do first.'

'Must I, sir? I feel defiled letting that Tommy swine paw me, sir.'

'Yes, you must. The Chief has ordered that you must go through with it. The police must find semen on your underclothing later when you report the rape.'

Her bottom lip trembled, as if she might cry. She looked across at the already fading photograph, framed with black crepe. It showed a serious young man, posing martially with spiked helmet and long bayoneted rifle. 'What must he think of me?' she quavered. 'I was always loyal to dear Heinrich, even when he was away at the front for so long.'

'Get on with it,' the 'Beast' said brutally, 'you're getting paid for it aren't you.'

She nodded tearfully.

Now as the squeak of oars got nearer, he retreated back into her 'best room'. He had his pistols and there were no houses very close to the woman's cottage. But he felt like using his hands. He looked down at the two hairy hams dangling between his knees. He flexed them, the knuckles cracking as he did so. The noise gave him pleasure. He squeezed them together as if tightening them around someone's throat. That gave him even more pleasure. His terrible face cracked into a parody of a smile. 'Yes, definitely the hands,' he whispered to himself.

Hurriedly Sparks tied up the little dinghy. He could see her outlined against the yellow light streaming from the open door of the kitchen. He grinned to himself. 'Can't wait for it,' he told himself happily. 'Lovely grub.' He touched his pocket. The packet of *'Players'* was still there. It was a little surprise for her. 'Bring her a couple o' bob on the black market,' he muttered, hurrying down the path, already feeling that old pleasurable thickening in his loins. 'Lovely grub,' he repeated to himself.

'Hello ducks,' he chortled. *'Ich liebe dich.'* He grabbed her in his arms and stuck his tongue deep inside her mouth. She wriggled and he said thickly, 'Now then, old girl. Don't go on fighting yersen – you know you love it.'

His hand slipped up her skirt and he felt between her legs. 'What did I tell yer. Come on, no time to waste. Let's get at it, wotcher!'

She let herself be led into the kitchen. Arm still around her, he kicked the door closed behind him, fumbling with his belt at the same time.

'Aber–' she began to protest. She didn't want to be found on her back when it happened.

But Sparks had no time for protests. He shoved her down on the sofa. 'Get them off,' he commanded hurriedly.

She didn't understand the words, but her eyes could tell her all too clearly what he wanted at this particular moment. She pulled down her knickers, keeping them hanging on her left leg.

'Hullo, hullo,' Sparks said cheerfully, 'that's a sight for sore eyes. Does me old mince-pies a world of good. Rightho, let's get to it, as the actress said to the bishop.' He whipped his own trousers down to his ankles and positioned himself above, his organ jutting out and swaying like a policeman's club. He saw the look in her eyes and misinterpreted it. 'Don't worry, luv,' he said, 'I'm particularly gentle with virgins.' He grunted and thrust his penis inside her.

Carefully, the 'Beast' peered through the gap in the door. The Tommy was on top of Frau Klose, his lean white buttocks pumping up and down vigorously and it was obvious to the 'Beast' that the bitch was enjoying it. Her legs were spread wide, high in the air, as if she couldn't get enough of him and her breath was coming in short, sharp, hectic gasps, her eyes screwed tight, her face twisted to one side, flushed and lathered in sweat.

'Lovely grub, eh,' the Tommy gasped. 'Bet you're enjoying this. They allus do.'

Noiselessly, the 'Beast' began to open the door wider, his anger mounting rapidly at the spectacle. The bitch had said she was a patriotic German who was only doing this in order to entrap the Tommy. But that wasn't true. It could have been a black Senegalese pumping himself into her. She wouldn't have cared, as long as he was a man.

He flexed his hands back and forth, as if he was itching to get them round the Englishman's throat and strangle the life out of him. On the couch the woman was beginning to moan, tossing her face from side to side in passion, her mouth gaping and stupid.

The 'Beast' growled deep in his throat. He swung the door open.

The Tommy reacted at once. He had felt the cold air coming from the cooler living room sweep across his naked rump. He stopped what he was doing immediately and flung himself from the woman, nimble and quick despite the fact that his trousers were around his ankles. 'What's the bleeding little game?' he demanded. Then he saw the 'Beast's' ruined face in the light of the single electric bulb and gasped. 'Christ Almighty, what a frigging mug!'

On the sofa the woman still lay with her legs spread and in the air, her eyes tightly shut.

Sparks took in the situation at once – wrongly. The fellow with the ugly mug was her husband. He'd been in situations like this before. He'd really been caught with his knickers down this time. In a swift gesture he pulled up his pants and faced up to the German who towered above him. Sparks wasn't afraid. He had been brought up in a tough neighbourhood, where he'd learned while still in short pants how to handle himself. Since then, he had learned a few more nasty tricks in waterfront bars all over the world with the Navy.

The 'Beast' growled something and reached out with his huge hairy paws. Sparks didn't hesitate. He lashed out with his right foot. The highly polished toe of his 'wrinkle-picker' caught the 'Beast' right in the crotch. He tumbled back, false teeth gaping from his shattered mouth.

The 'Beast' growled low and threatening. He struggled back up. Sparks looked anxious. A kick in the groin like that would have put most men out. Not this monster. Behind him the German woman gave a little scream. She pulled her frock down and held her hands to her eyes as if she couldn't face the horror to come.

Sparks' quick cockney brain raced. He knew if the monster once caught hold of him, he'd had it. His best bet was to get out of the cottage and do a runner. Desperately he looked around for some way of stopping the monster so that he could do so. His eye fell on the pepper pot on the kitchen table. He seized it and in one and the same motion sent its contents flying in the direction of his attacker.

The 'Beast' yelled with sudden pain. He clawed at his suddenly burning eyes, sneezing violently as he did so. He shook his head crazily, trying to drive away the burning.

Sparks was off. 'Bye bye birdie' he sang out and then he was out of the door in a flash, telling himself that had been a close one. He ran towards where he had tied up the dinghy, heart leaping with sudden joy with the thought that he had got away with it again. Luck had been on his side once more.

Behind him he heard the monster stagger through the open kitchen door and shout something in German.

Sparks paid no attention. He was concentrating totally on reaching that boat and setting off into safe mid-stream. Suddenly, he felt himself flying. He had stumbled over something in the darkness. 'Gordon Bennett!' he yelled and sprawled full length, the wind knocked out of him.

He heard heavy feet pounding behind him. Desperately he raised himself, feeling a little sick. He started to run again. Too late. A tremendous blow hit him in the small of the back. He went down again to his knees under the impact. Next instant two great hairy paws clamped around his throat and he heard the monster grunt, *'Die Englishman!'*

They were the last words he ever heard...

FIVE

'Sparks is missing,' CPO Ferguson announced at the door of the little wardroom.

Smith looked up sharply from the inevitable pink gin. In a couple of hours they would be taking out the nightly patrol and this was his last drink. 'Missing did you say? Missing where?'

'Hey, you, Kerrigan,' CPO Ferguson barked to Ginger, who was standing behind, looking very uncomfortable. 'Tell the officer what ye kens. At the double!'

'Well, sir,' Ginger said, with unusual hesitancy, 'Sparks has got hissen a tart – er I mean a woman.' He swallowed hard.

'Get on with it,' Smith snapped. 'What's the woman got to do with it?'

'She's got a house on the other side of the Rhine and he took the dinghy to – er see her.'

Smith groaned and Dickie Bird said, 'The ruddy fool. Doesn't he know he could land himself in a lot of hot water over there?'

'Yessir,' Ginger agreed. 'But yer know what Sparks is with the women. He always fancies his chances something rotten.'

'But why do you think he's missing?'

Smith interrupted urgently.

'Well, sir, he should have been back an hour ago. Last time he did it,' Ginger actually blushed, 'well you know what I mean, sir – in two hours flat. That's his style. He allus sez he's a Three F man–'

'A what?'

'Three F, sir, and sometimes a Four-F man – find 'em, feel 'em and fuck 'em, if you'll pardon my French – and then sometimes forget 'em. Four F's.' Ginger saw the warning look on Smith's tense face and he hurried on. 'Well, he hasn't come back and me and my oppo Billy thinks something's happened to him on the other bank.'

'Do you know the house where this woman lives?' Smith snapped, brain racing electrically.

'Yessir. I've seen it a couple of times in daylight and I've seen her as well. Big blonde – plenty o' meat on her.'

Smith was no longer listening to Ginger. Instead he turned to CPO Ferguson and said hurriedly, 'Stand the crew to, Chiefie. I'm going to hop on the phone and call Major McIntyre. Dickie,' he drained the rest of his pink gin in one gulp, 'You take over till I come back.'

'Of course, Smithie, but what are you going to do, old bean?'

'Go across and find Sparks. I know he's been a blithering idiot. But he is a good chap and he's one of us, isn't he?'

'Of course, Smithie. Quite agree. Cut along then and I'll get this sorted out.'

'And Dickie,' Smith paused at the door of the wardroom.

'Yes?'

'Break out the firearms. You never know in Germany.' And with that he was gone…

Half an hour later, they were underway, chugging across the Rhine at low speed. McIntyre had brought Dietz with him and when CPO Ferguson handed him a pistol, the former quavered. 'I don't like weapons. Do I have to take it?'

CPO Ferguson snorted something about 'bloody squareheads', and Smith said, straining his eyes at the gloom, 'I'm determined to get my chap back. If we have to use force, then,' he shrugged and left the rest of his sentence unfinished.

McIntyre nodded his agreement, head huddled in the collar of his greatcoat, for he had had no time to change into civilian clothes.

'You might be right, Smith. Somehow I have the feeling that this Sparks fellow of yours has got himself in some kind of trouble. Not with husbands or anything of that kind, but with von Horn and his mob.'

'My sentiments exactly,' Smith said.

'Sir!' an urgent voice called from the bow.

It was Ginger Kerrigan.

'What is it?'

'There's the house, sir. To the right a bit.'

Hastily Smith swung up his night glasses. A small cottage came into view. There was a yellow light in the window. It was occupied all right. He nodded to CPO Ferguson at the wheel and he spun the *Swordfish* round a little and set course for the German woman's house.

'All right, stand by,' Smith called softly, as the boat nosed its way to the opposite bank. 'Ginger and Billy look lively. You're coming with us. Dickie, you take charge of the *Swordfish*. Keep your eyes skinned.'

'Like the proverbial tin of peeled tomatoes,' Dickie Bird answered cheerfully.

A moment later, the *Swordfish* heaved to and McIntyre and a highly nervous Dietz followed McIntyre, Smith and the two ratings ashore. Smith paused and scanned the bank to left and right, giving the water quick flashes of his torchbeam. 'No sign of the dinghy, Major,' he said after a moment.

'Strange,' McIntyre muttered.

'Yes, very. We ought to have seen him if he'd come back in it. And he should have very definitely seen *us*.'

'Yes, Smith, I agree. Come on, let's have a look-see at the Hun woman's house.'

Carefully, trying to make as little noise as possible, they moved up the garden in the darkness. Suddenly Billy Bennett stumbled and went down on his knees. He mumbled, 'Sorry, sir, fell over some bleeding thing in the dark.' He stopped short and then said urgently, 'Sir, I think I've found summat.'

'What?' Smith demanded in irritation. The fat rating would wake up the whole neighbourhood if he went on babbling like that.

'His cap.'

'Whose cap?'

'Sparks.'

Smith grabbed for the cap that the fat soldier was holding. He gave it a flash of the torch. It was the one he had bought for the crew. But even without the light he would have recognized it all right. The cap gave off a powerful odour of that violet pomade that Sparks used on his hair. 'Come on,' he hissed urgently. 'I think Sparks is in trouble – bad trouble!'

They hurried forward towards the yellow light of the cottage, each man wrapped in a cocoon of his own thoughts and apprehension. Sparks had been a typical cockney matelot, a bit of a show-off who talked too much, but he had been a good shipmate as well. None of them wished him any harm.

Smith held up his hand. They stopped automatically. He bent and peered through the kitchen window. Despite the lateness of the hour, there was someone inside the kitchen; he could hear that.

A woman was sitting at the kitchen table, a shawl thrown about her plump naked shoulders. She was slumped there in the classic pose of despair, hands holding her bowed head, shoulders heaving as she sobbed softly, as if her heart were broken. Smith flashed a look around the rest of the kitchen. Nothing. No sign of Sparks. 'Ginger,' he hissed.

Ginger Kerrigan came to his side and peered through the window with him.

'Is that her, Ginger?'

'Yessir. That's her,' Ginger whispered back.

Smith turned and looked at McIntyre. He nodded and drew his revolver and pointed the muzzle to his own brawny chest. That meant he was to lead. Smith nodded his agreement.

McIntyre took the door handle in his hand and tried it gently. The door didn't open. It was locked. He didn't hesitate. He moved back, raised his boot and slammed it at the panel with all his strength. The lock snapped and the door flew open. Next instant he was inside, revolver held menacingly at his hip, ready to fire at the first sign of trouble.

The woman gasped with shock. The shawl fell from her shoulders to reveal the naked breasts beneath. '*Was machen–*' she began, trembling with fear.

–'Shut up,' McIntyre cut her short brutally in German, as Smith and Ginger, followed by Dietz, pushed their way into the kitchen, while Billy Bennett kept watch outside. 'Where's the Englishman?'

'The Englishman,' the woman quavered stupidly and then she began to sob again.

McIntyre hit her across the face. 'Stop that, woman. I'm asking you a question – where's the Englishman? Now, quick, or it will be the worse for you.'

Shocked, her pale face bearing the red marks of his fingers, the woman choked. 'He's gone … the Englishman.'

'Where?' McIntyre demanded and added for Dietz's benefit. 'Quick, have a gander at the rest of the place.'

He looked at the woman again, as Smith watched him and told himself that the Canadian was a tough bastard. He didn't pull his punches, even with women. 'All right now, come on, what happened to the Englishman?'

Her lips trembling, as if she might break out crying again at any moment, she quavered, 'The other man, he went after him.'

'What other man?'

'The one with the terrible face from the north. The authorities sent him. I was to have the Englishman in the house when he came…'

McIntyre looked hard at Smith and the latter nodded his understanding. Sparks had been lured to this place. The woman had been the bait. The man from the north would only be one of von Horn's people. But why Sparks and what had happened to the handsome cockney?

'Where did he go after him – this man from the north?' McIntyre demanded, voice hard and relentless.

She shrugged a little helplessly. 'I only know he wanted the Englishman's boat. What he was going to do with it–'

–'Sir ... sir...' It was Billy Bennett, standing in the open door, fat face flushed an angry red. 'I've found ... found him,' he gasped.

'Sparks?' Smith snapped, iron in his voice.

'Yessir. Poor sod's bin strangled to death.'

'Come on,' McIntyre cried. 'Dietz, see what you can squeeze out of the dame about this man from the north.' Together they piled out of the room and followed Billy Bennett, who was cursing angrily to himself about what he would do to the killer if he ever got his hands on him.

Sparks was lying huddled behind a pile of logs, his head tilted to one side at an unnatural angle. Smith, playing his torch on the ashen face, could see the trickle of blood which had come out of the side of his mouth and the eyes which bulged out of their sockets. McIntyre, who seemed to know about such things, said softly, 'The poor bastard's been strangled to death. Look at those bruise marks on his neck. The man from the north must have the strength of an ox – or a madman.'

Smith shook his head sadly. Then he pulled himself together. 'All right, Ginger and Billy, will you please gather him up. We're taking him back with us. I'm not going to allow one of the *Swordfish's* crew to–'

There was a sharp crack like a twig being snapped underfoot in a hot dry summer. Scarlet flame stabbed the gloom. A bullet howled off the logs, showering the dead man's face with wood splinters. 'Christ,' McIntyre yelled. 'Someone's firing at us!'

That first shot acted, seemingly, as a signal. Another shot followed – and another. They came from behind the little cottage and were obviously being fired from pistols.

Angrily Smith reacted, his mind full of the brutal murder of Sparks. He fired off a wild burst in the direction from which the pistol shots were coming. There was a yelp of pain. Something heavy fell to the ground. Another voice yelled in rage. A small egg-like object came whirling out of the darkness. 'Duck!' Smith cried urgently.

The grenade exploded only feet away. Red-hot, glowing shards of metal flew everywhere. Smith felt something hot sting him on the side of his jaw. He yelped. Next to him McIntyre cried, 'Fuck this for a tale!' He pulled out his automatic and started blasting away.

Behind him Ginger and Bennett staggered on with the body of Sparks.

Now, with McIntyre and Smith giving the little party covering fire, they headed for the waiting *Swordfish,* while their attackers edged closer, clearly outlined in the scarlet stabs of flame. Smith didn't have time to count them, but they clearly outnumbered their group by at least three to one. Further off he could hear the distinctive horn of a German police car hurrying towards the scene of the shooting and he didn't need a crystal ball to know on whose side the police would be. If they didn't make it to the boat soon, it was pretty clear they wouldn't survive to see another sunrise. 'Get cracking,' he urged the panting two ratings carrying the corpse. 'Come on... They're getting closer.'

Suddenly there was the thunderous clatter of a machine gun. White tracer sailed over their heads in lethal fury and slammed into the first line of their attackers. They were bowled in a mess of flailing limbs, screaming in pain – and then the Smith party was clambering aboard the *Swordfish* frantically, carrying with them their burden of death. They had made it.

SIX

Saturday.

It was three in the afternoon. In Cologne the stores were closed and hush had descended upon the Rhenish city. Now the Roman Catholic Church would rule till Monday morning. Anyone who was foolish enough to use a lawn-mower would be reported immediately to the police for having disturbed the pre-Sunday religious silence. A housewife dare not hang out a solitary towel. No children played in the streets. Even the brothels in the red light district behind the station were subdued. No music was allowed.

But in the GOC's riverside villa no one paid any attention to the restrictions of the Archbishop of Cologne. In the hall, a string quartet from West Yorks played the popular tunes of the war, selections from *'Chu Chin Chow'* and the like, while hearty, slightly bandy officers from the 8th Hussars talked of the old days. Attentive mess waiters in white jackets circulated with silver trays heavy with champagne and whisky.

The GOC, in particular, was in good spirits. There was not even the slightest hint that he was aware that this was the day when he was supposed to be assassinated. He 'circulated' constantly, talking about the pre-war days at the cavalry school at Curragh, how 'old Jumbo Webster' went 'arse over bollocks' in the riding ring and what that 'tough little Irish riding master had said afterwards, all punctuated with plenty of 'haws-haws' and frequent tugging at his long, straggly, cavalry moustache.

Outside, the atmosphere was different. In the distance the German police in their tall leather helmets and green overcoats had sealed off the whole area, turning back walkers and people exercising their dogs along the Rhine. Closer at hand, little patrols of the West York company, now commanded temporarily by McIntyre, explored the grounds. Men armed with long sticks poked inside the bushes and the lower branches of the splendid oaks, while others covered them with loaded rifles.

McIntyre was here, there and everywhere, loaded revolver in both pockets of his rumpled tunic, a worried look on his tough, craggy face. For he knew that the villa was too big and the grounds too extensive for one hundred per cent security. Why, he told himself, a sniper in any one of those oaks could pot off the GOC every time he exposed himself in one of the tall french windows of the villa. He and his men could not relax the vigilance for a second.

Off the bank of the Rhine, the *Swordfish* cruised back and forth at a snail's pace, every man on watch lining the deck and acting as lookouts. Two hours before they had found the missing dinghy. But it was empty and a thorough search of it had revealed little of the man who had killed poor Sparks and made off with it. 'All that we know, Dickie,' Smith had concluded finally, 'is that the killer is on our side of the Rhine. But where?' He had shrugged a little helplessly.

Tension was high, for even dullards like Billy Bennett, usually more concerned with filling his ample stomach than politics, knew what was at stake. If the unknown German succeeded in killing the GOC, there could be a revolution. As Ginger Kerrigan had said gloomily, 'If the balloon does go up, Billy, I hope the skipper'll get us out of here right sharpish. I wouldn't like to be stranded here.'

'Amen to that,' Billy had agreed sombrely.

At four, with the light beginning to go, McIntyre came over to the *Swordfish* for five minutes. Eagerly he downed the pink gin which Smith offered him and reported, 'The Hussars chaps are beginning to drift off, which is all to the good. Perhaps then I can convince the GOC to keep away from those windows. I've heard from C too,' he added. 'He's making representations to the German government in Berlin through the PM of course – not that the Welsh Wizard' – he meant Lloyd George, the Prime Minister – 'will be very effective. The latest from his office is "Kiss the Hun and kill the Bolshy".' He frowned darkly and under other circumstances, Dickie Bird would have been inclined to laugh and make a weak joke. Not now. The situation was obviously too serious.

'What does C want the Germans to do?' Smith asked.

'Well, he's told the Welsh Wizard a little about this affair here. He wants the PM to put pressure on the Huns in Berlin to stop this Hitler before the balloon really goes up.' McIntyre sucked his teeth. 'Don't know how far the PM'll get though. The Jerry government are a weak bunch.' He reached for his cap. 'Ah well, better get back and check that those West Yorks don't go back marching to attention with their rifles at the slope.'

The hours passed leadenly. Now it was completely dark. No noise, not even that of the trams, came from Cologne. It was all buried in pre-Sunday religious gloom. The lights still burned brightly at the villa though and the last guests had still not departed. On the wind they could still hear the West Yorks' quarter scraping away, playing 'Pack up your troubles in yer old kitbag,' which occasioned Billy Bennett, whose stomach was rumbling loudly, to remark, 'I wish I could pack up my troubles and get down to the galley, I'm ruddy well starving.'

At six, Smith stood down half the watch so that they could go below and get something to eat and a hot drink, warning the men, 'Half an hour that's all, then you're back on deck to relieve the other half watch. Off you go.'

At seven, it started to rain, a thin, bitter drizzle which chilled to the bone so that the men on the open deck huddled in their oilskins, stamping their feet to keep the chill out, wishing they were back in the warm fug of the galley.

Smith wiped the moisture from his face and cursed. 'Just the damned weather we need at this moment, Dickie.'

'You can say that again, Smithie. Can't see a hand before my face. Jolly bad show.'

'Well, we've got to live with it. Let's get in closer to the river bank and use the searchlight. We'll sweep it along systematically.'

Dickie wasn't so enthusiastic. 'But do you really think, old bean,' he said, 'that this Hun murderer chappie will approach the house from that direction?'

'I don't really know, Dickie. What do you suggest?'

'I've been thinking about it since the rain started. Visibility is about zero and I don't think we're doing much good out here. I think we'd do more good if we joined McIntyre with foot patrols. I think it'd be better for the chaps too. At least they'd be moving and keeping a bit warmer.'

Smith considered for a moment. Then he made his decision. Thus it was that the *Swordfish* was tying up just as Hopkins drove the GOC's Rolls Royce out of the villa's drive to pick up the General's last visitor of that fateful Saturday night.

Kati von Duckwitz stood naked in front of the full length mirror in her bedroom and admired her young body. She had just emerged from her bath and her ivory skin glowed a faint, warm pink. She turned and looked over her shoulder, admiring her shapely back and pert buttocks. Happily she blew herself a kiss and taking up the large powder puff, dipped it in the scented powder and began to dust herself with it, enjoying the sensation as she spread the powder over her breasts and along her erect nipples.

She had always felt like this. When she had gone to Cheltenham Ladies College back in 1919, paid for by her rich Swiss relatives, she had not enjoyed any of the 'crushes' that the other girls had on one another. Not because she was the ex-enemy, the first German girl in the college since the war, but because she enjoyed her own body more than she would have done that of another girl. Alone in her own cubicle in the dormitory at night, listening to the secretive giggles and moans of girls in bed together, she had felt nothing, neither lust nor sorrow that she didn't have a 'little friend'. She had been sufficient to herself and always would be. She wet the finger of her free hand and inserted it gently in her vagina. She gave a little shudder of delight and told herself that was the best way of all. No man alive could ever give her that kind of thrill.

But she needed men all the same. Even she was forced to pander to their silly little perversions, particularly the older ones. For men meant money and power. She had long realized that, and she was determined never to be poor again. Through men – and bed – she could achieve her aim, the restoration of the von Duckwitz estate in all its former glory. It was a duty she owed to her ancestors.

She stopped playing with herself and concentrated on her dressing, knowing that this night would be one of the most momentous in her life. She slipped on the sheer silk black drawers the General had brought her on his last leave in Paris. One of the new fangled brassieres, also in black and from

Paris, followed. She sat on the bed, still admiringly her body in the mirror and pulled on black stockings, which fastened with red garters – the General was always very specific on what she should wear underneath. More than once he had sent her an itemized list prior to their Saturday night mating, instructing her on what she should clothe herself in. Finally the frock came, one of those new very short ones imported from New York, 'the flapper look', the papers were calling it. It barely came to her knees and would have cost a fortune on the German market. Fortunately with the sovereigns the General gave her she had been able to buy it for a song.

She pulled it down snugly.

Now she was ready to look out of her window. She crossed to the big window overlooking the park opposite. It was raining and visibility was bad, but he was there all right. He was lounging against a lamp, hat pulled well down over his face so that she could not see it. But she knew it was him all right. She had been sent a full-length photograph of the man the previous week.

She nodded her approval and went back into the bedroom. Her purse lay on the dressing table. She opened it and looked the contents over. There was the new Swiss passport, a bundle of currency, French, Swiss and British, and beyond that – the little pearl-handled pistol.

She smiled at herself in the dressing table mirror and then, content, she sat down and began to brush her short bob, which the delighted General said always made her look 'no more than a schoolgirl – and a very naughty one at that.'

Her smile broadened at the memory. Just how naughty she was the silly old fool could hardly conceive. She continued to brush her hair, while down below the big man waited in the rain, the drops running down his ruined face unheeded…

Trooper Hopkins drove the big Rolls Royce carefully. The General was a stickler for appearances and he couldn't afford to have some fool squarehead bumping into it in this terrible weather. Not that they were about much. He turned off the Hansaring into the street where she lived, just opposite the new park created by the burgomaster Adenauer, the General's friend, who looked like a wizened monkey. The street was deserted, the cobbles gleaming in the rain in the headlights of the big car. All to the good, Hopkins told himself. He knew trouble was expected for this night and he, personally, didn't want to be involved in it.

The General could get on with his whore-mongering later on – and what else was to come. He'd be quite happy to put his feet up, drinking his 'Bass' and smoking his pipe, and having a good old read at the *'Pink 'Un'*, though it was pretty impossible to use any of the racing tips it gave its readers.

'Number Sixty-Nine,' he read out the number of the apartment house where she had her flat. He sniffed. 'Right kind of number for her nibs,' he said aloud, speaking to himself in the fashion of lonely men. He patted the pocket of his immaculate tunic and felt the comforting feel of a pistol it in. Hopkins was what he called 'a belt and braces man'; never took chances. He looked left and right. The place was empty. He nodded his approval. Putting on his cap, he strode through the rain to the door of the apartment house. He pressed the bell and waited, cap off, ready to greet her with the usual, 'Good evening, Miss. The General expects you.' He sniffed again and told himself the General was expecting a little bit of the other as well.

Upstairs, Kati von Duckwitz heard the bell ring. She was already fully dressed and ready, purse under her arm. But she forced herself to count off the minutes to give him time. Then when five minutes were up, she opened her door and prepared to descend to the waiting car.

SEVEN

'Okay,' McIntyre agreed, wiping the raindrops off his tense face, 'I guess you're right. You can't do much good on the river in damned weather like this–' He stopped suddenly. The General's car was returning, turning slowly into the drive to the villa, as Hopkins worked the windscreen wipers manually.

McIntyre said, 'Oh, it's the GOC's girlfriend.'

Next to him, Dickie Bird grinned despite the rain, and said, 'Heaven help a sailor on a night like this! God, what wouldn't I give to tuck myself around a nice nubile female – even if she is a Hun.'

'Shut up,' Smith said and McIntyre said, 'You never know. A Hun is a Hun.'

He stepped into the drive and held up his hand. In time, Hopkins spotted him and, pulling up the Rolls Royce, turned on the interior lighting. Smith and Bird saw a very pretty blonde sitting in the back, doll-like, with a white powdered face and huge baby blue eyes.

'The General's guest, sir,' Hopkins said – and sniffed significantly.

‘What’s up, Trooper?’ McIntyre rasped. ‘Got a cold?’

Hopkins thought it best not to reply. Instead, he waited patiently, while McIntyre touched his hand to his battered cap in cold politeness, ‘Good evening, miss,’ he said, and swept his hard gaze around the Rolls’ interior. He nodded to Hopkins. ‘All right, Trooper, carry on.’

‘Thank you, sir. Good night, sir.’

McIntyre nodded again and the big car carried on, with the girl not deigning to notice McIntyre’s presence, though her heart was beating like a trip-hammer.

Dickie whistled softly through his teeth. ‘I say,’ he gushed, ‘that one’s worth a sin or two.’

‘Not for the likes of you,’ Smith said firmly. ‘Reserved for general officers.’

‘There’s no justice in this world,’ Dickie moaned.

‘Knock it off,’ McIntyre interrupted harshly. The strain was beginning to tell on him, Smith told himself. ‘You fellers can form the inner perimeter right around the villa,’ he decided. ‘If I had my way I’d have the lot of you *inside* the place. But the General won’t buy that, of course. He wants to be alone with his beloved.’

‘Can’t blame him,’ Dickie said, a little mournfully, as the sudden gust of wind lashed his face with ice-cold rain.

'What do you think?' Smith asked urgently. 'Do you think von Horn has called it off? I mean our security is pretty damn tight.'

McIntyre shook his head. 'No. We know the killer's on this side of the Rhine. The silly old fart's alone in the house with his woman and Trooper Hopkins. The field's still wide open...'

The 'Beast' crouched in the boot of the Rolls Royce, listening intently as the woman got out and the Tommy driving her said something he couldn't understand. He heard the car being put into gear once more. It moved off very slowly. If von Horn's information was correct, the car would now drive to the garage at the back of the house where the chauffeur had his quarters. A minute passed. The car halted again. He heard the clatter of a steel shutter being raised. He nodded his approval. The door of a garage. Von Horn's information had been correct. The car moved inside. The door was shut. The engine was turned off.

He heard the chauffeur cough and then the crunch of his boots on a concrete floor. A door was opened. That would be the door to the stairs leading to the chauffeur's quarters above the garage. It was now or never. Gently, the 'Beast' raised the lid of the boot, grateful for the perfection of the big luxury car. It made absolutely no noise. He stepped out and peered through the yellow gloom. The door to the stairs was still open. The chauffeur had not yet closed it. He darted forward. He had to get up those stairs and into the villa.

Heavy boots were coming downstairs once more. The chauffeur was coming back to lock the car and the door. The 'Beast' tensed, big hands at the ready.

Trooper Hopkins came through the door, a bottle of 'Bass' already open. He had been craving for a drink of beer for hours now. That had been the first thing he had done upstairs – had a good swig at the 'Bass'. 'Can't stand that foreign stuff,' he had said to himself, speaking aloud in the manner of lonely men. 'Like gnat's piss.'

He stopped short. 'Hey, what the devil are you doing there?' he cried.

Suddenly he saw the 'Beast's' mutilated face. *'Christ Almighty!'* he exclaimed. He dropped the bottle. It shattered on the concrete floor. Madly, he tried to reach for the revolver in the pocket of his tunic.

The 'Beast' didn't give him a chance. With an animal grunt that came from deep down inside him, he sprang forward. His hands found and tensed around the soldier's neck. Hopkins gasped, face suddenly contorted with unreasoning, overwhelming fear. He tried to break that murderous grip. To no avail! The 'Beast' exerted yet more pressure. Hopkin's face turned purple. His eyes bulged from his head. Desperately, furiously, Hopkins tried to break free before it was too late. Already red stars were exploding in front of his eyes. His heart was thumping away furiously. He'd be unconscious in a few moments.

The 'Beast' didn't give him a chance. 'Die,' he hissed through gritted teeth, '*die!*'

Suddenly, startlingly, Hopkins went limp, his eyes rolling upwards.

The 'Beast' was taking no chances. He kept up that tremendous pressure for a minute longer. Then slowly and gently he lowered Hopkins to the floor and felt for a pulse. There wasn't one. The Englishman was dead. The 'Beast' licked his suddenly dry lips. He felt a sense of elation. He was inside the villa, alone with the General and the woman...

'Well, how do you like it, Alex?' Kati von Duckwitz asked, after the General had very gallantly kissed her hand.

'Exceedingly pretty, my dear,' the General said, his usual pale face flushed with the afternoon's drinking with the officers of the 8th Hussars. 'Most becoming.'

She laughed, showing those beautiful, white teeth of hers. Seemingly full of the exuberance of youth, she twirled round on the toes of her high-heel shoes. The short skirt furled outwards and upwards and the General had a momentary glimpse of taut young buttocks clad in sheer black silk. He almost spilled his glass of champagne at the sight. 'What a delightfully naughty young filly you are, m'dear!' he exclaimed.

She tweaked his raddled cheek playfully, 'And I hope my general is going to be very naughty too tonight?' she simpered.

'By Gad,' the GOC said heartily, 'you do do something for an old chap like me. But I'm neglecting my duties. Let me get you a glass of champagne.'

'I'd love one,' she said, all smiles and fluttering eyelashes. 'I'd rather like to get a little tipsy.'

'Well, I'm the chap to get you in that delightful state, m'dear. Here you are. Bottoms up. What?'

'Bottoms up,' she echoed and raised the *flute*. 'But not just yet, what?' she mimicked his cavalryman's drawl quite well and he exclaimed, 'Capital, m'dear. Capital. You've got me off to a T. Now then, be a dear and come and sit on my lap. It's cold and rainy outside. And old buffer like me needs a bit of warming up on a night like this, what.'

Obediently she slipped on to his lap, his polished cavalry boots creaked as he took the extra weight. Her short skirt rode up again to reveal a delightful red silk garter holding up the sheer black silk stocking.

'I say,' he said, feeling a stirring in his aged loins already. 'That red garter does something for a chap.'

Playfully, she hooked her fingers inside the garter and pulled the elastic up, allowing it then to slip and slap against her taut thigh.

He chuckled with delight. 'I say, Kati, m'dear. I think we're going to have a perfectly ripping time tonight, what.'

'Oh, perfectly ripping, what,' she mimicked him again with a smile. Inside her, a hard little voice said, *'Yes, and for the last time, too...'*

'I say, Dickie,' Smith exclaimed angrily, as a fresh burst of bitterly cold raindrops slashed him across the face, 'Bugger this for a tale. Those brown jobs,' he meant the men of the West Yorks patrolling the river bank somewhat noisily, 'are trained for this sort of thing. They enjoy being out in all sorts of weathers and being miserable. Well, we're not. Come on.'

'Where are we going, old bean?' Dickie asked, feeling pretty miserable and cold himself.

'Inside the villa.' He indicated the house behind them. 'Look, the old codger's upstairs already with his girlfriend. The lights are out up there. He won't even know we're inside. Come on, I've had enough.'

Together the wet, dispirited crew of the *Swordfish,* their oilskins glistening in the bitter rain, filed inside the big hall. Ginger and the rest gazed around at the oil paintings and portraits which adorned the walls with something like apprehension.

Dickie saw the looks and said, 'Don't worry. It ain't the General's either. He's just borrowed it from the Huns. But don't go making a mess of his floor. Generals don't like you to do things like that.'

Smith turned to CPO Ferguson, 'Chiefie, you're in charge of the chaps out here. Mr Bird and me will have a look around on the ground floor. Test the windows and the like.' He frowned. 'Funny, you'd think that the GOC would have servants and the like, more than just that one groom.'

'Ay, he does,' CPO Ferguson said, face set in a look of disapproval. 'When he has his fancy woman in, they're all packed off to the annexe at yon back o' the huis. Early.'

Smith grinned. 'You're a real old puritan, Chiefie, do you know.'

'Well, I dinna rightly ken what yon word means,' Ferguson growled, 'but if it means I dinna like our generals carryin' on with Jerry fancy woman – then I am.'

Now Smith and Bird wandered through the silent house, checking to see whether the many doors and windows were securely locked. All was silent save for the howl of the wind and the rattle of the rain-lashed windows. Occasionally there were the sounds of muted laughter and once something, which could have been a bottle, falling on the floor from above. But that was all. In the dim light, the bulbs flickering every now and again because of the storm, there was something a little eerie about the place. More than once Smith was tempted to look behind him to see if there was really anyone lurking there in the shadows, but he caught himself just in time. Now when they spoke, the two of them lowered their voices, as if they might be overheard. Why they did not know. For they knew there was no one else on this floor.

'It comes,' Dickie Bird summed it up in a whisper as they turned into the kitchens, 'from reading far too many ghost stories at Harrow-on-the-Hill after lights out.'

Smith chuckled softly. 'I suppose you're right,' he said aloud. But at the back of his mind a hard little voice said, 'It's not that at all. It was the look on poor old Sparks' face. The monster who murdered him must have the strength of a maniac.' The small hairs at the back of Smith's head suddenly stood erect and he shivered.

'Somebody walk over your grave?' Dickie quipped.

'Something like that.' Smith forced

himself to be business-like. ‘All right, cut the cackle. Let’s have a look-see at those windows.’

EIGHT

The General lay on the big bed, legs wide apart and completely naked save for his socks, his teeth in a glass on the bedside table, gasping urgently. 'What a cunning little minx, you are!' he panted, his skinny white body glazed in sweat, as she worked upon him busily. 'Be-gad, why can't damned wives be like this. *Oh!'* his whole body trembled as her cunning little fingers gave him another delicious thrill. 'I swear,' he panted … 'I swear, I could die happy this very night!'

She looked at the General in disgust. His eyes were screwed up like those of a child, deep in some beautiful sleep, and not wanting to wake up to the awful realities of the nursery. She grinned. What a prophetic statement he had just made! She gave him a last tug, slapped his testicles lightly, and wiped the vaseline, with which his penis was smeared, off her hand onto the towel on the other side of the bed. 'General,' she breathed, thrusting her wet tongue into his ancient ear until he squirmed with pleasure, 'I shall have to go and make a pi-pi now. You have made me *so* excited, that I can't hold myself ... you understand – much longer.'

He opened his eyes and stared at her naked body. 'Must you, *now?*' he asked miserably.

'Yes, my general,' she said, thrusting her hands between her legs in the manner of a little girl.

He stared down at his loins. The effect was already beginning to wear off.

She saw his look. 'Don't worry. We shall do that delightful thing all over again until it stands. This time, however, much naughtier.' She opened her mouth and ran her pink tongue around her lips suggestively.

'Oh, I say,' he gasped. 'Do you really mean–'

'Now close your eyes and rest for a moment. You'll need all your strength for what I am going to give you this night.'

'Oh, will I?' The General screwed up his eyes, as if his very life depended upon it.

She didn't waste any time. She picked up her shoes and clothes from the chair beside the bed. On tip-toe she went out to the large ornate bathroom, with its gold taps and lavatory set on a marble pedestal, as if it were a throne. On the bed the panting General continued to keep his eyes closed, no doubt allowing his mind to dwell on the delightful things she would do to him with her cunning mouth when she returned.

Hurriedly she dressed, going through her

instructions as she did so. Time was now of the essence. He would already be in the upper storey. Now he needed the signal. She remembered von Horn's instructions. 'Once he had done the job, Gracious Miss, you will deal with him. His dead body must be found next to that of the Tommy. Your part in his death will naturally be hushed up by the English. They are a prudish race. It wouldn't look good for the dead general to be found with a mistress, German and a third of his age to boot. Once the English police have been dealt with, you fade out of the scene and go straight to Switzerland, as planned. But the main thing is we have our symbol, which will help to create a new Germany.' At the memory of those words, her eyes glistened fanatically. *'A new Germany!'* she whispered fervently to herself, 'in which all this Jewish decadence and perversion will vanish.' She pulled the lavatory chain once, waited till the cistern flooded again, and pulled it once more.

It was the signal...

The 'Beast' heard the signal as he crouched on the balcony outside the General's bedroom. He had seen what had gone on before and had wondered how a well-born German woman, even if it was done for the cause of the Fatherland, could indulge in such perversion. It had made his blood boil. More than once, he had muttered, '*Schweinerei* – such piggery–' and had forced himself not to break through the window and carry out his mission there and then.

Now she had given the signal from the lavatory. It meant the coast was clear. He could finally do what he had come so far to do. Tomorrow the whole of Germany would ring to the news. The English Army Commander had been assassinated by a patriotic German. It would be the call to arms!

Gently, almost noiselessly, he inserted the blade of his knife into the gap between the windows underneath the catch. On the bed the naked old man lay motionless, eyes still tightly screwed together. He was still waiting. The 'Beast' gave that terrible, mutilated smile of his. The old man would be surprised. What he would receive in a moment would not be love, perverted as it was, but *death!*

Carefully, he started to raise the catch with the blade of his penknife...

Dickie had just checked the kitchen door and was standing outside under the canopy, watching the raindrops coming down in bitter relentlessness, when his nose wrinkled at the smell. It wasn't from the kitchen, but from above him. He frowned in bewilderment, only half realising why he was bewildered.

'Shut the door,' Smith inside the kitchen

ordered. 'It's bloody cold, you know.'

For a moment, Bird didn't respond and Smith snapped, 'What's the matter, Dickie? Have you got wax in your ears?'

Dickie shook his head like someone coming out of a heavy sleep. 'No. There's a funny pong.'

'What do you mean – a funny pong?'

'Up there.' Suddenly Dickie Bird was one hundred per cent alert. 'You know, it's the way the Huns pong. That black tobacco they smoke and that funny hard ersatz soap of theirs, which doesn't have any perfume in it–'

–'But the only Hun in this house at this moment is the General's whore and presumably she's deep down underneath the feathers by – Christ, do you think it's the killer?' Smith snorted urgently.

'Could well be, and he's up there somewhere. I–'

He didn't finish. Smith pushed him to one side and peered upwards through the falling rain, straining his eyes urgently. Suddenly he saw the dark shape crouched there on the balcony, outlined as a stark menacing black by the light coming from the General's bedroom. 'Hey, you, what are you up to?'

A flash of scarlet stabbed the rain-sodden darkness. Smith ducked as a bullet howled off the stonework a foot from his head. 'It's him, Dickie!' he cried. *'The killer!'*

‘Oh, my sainted aunt!’ Dickie yelled and dashed inside, yelling at the top of his voice. ‘Stand to ... *it’s him!*’

‘Lash up and stow,’ Ginger responded first. ‘The squarehead’s up there with his nibs and the tart. Come on, lads!’ He started to pelt up the stairs which led to the bedrooms, followed by the others, already brandishing their coshes and revolvers.

Outside, Smith, narrowing his eyes against the rain, aimed and fired.

The dark shape jerked convulsively. Smith had hit him. But the young officer had not reckoned with the enormous strength of the ‘Beast’. Despite the blood pumping in a scarlet arc from his wounded shoulder, he smashed through the window and landed on his toes inside.

The GOC shot up from the big bed. ‘What the hell’s going–’ He stopped short when he saw the mutilated monster crouching there. At once he realized that the Colonial had been right all along. This man was about to kill him. Desperately he searched around for something to defend himself. There was nothing! All he could do was to try to reason with the man, for already he could hear the many feet pounding up the stairs.

‘It’s no use,’ he stuttered. ‘You haven’t a chance. Give up while you...’ his words trailed away. He could see that he wasn’t making any impression on the monster.

Slowly, the blood still pouring from his wounded shoulder, the 'Beast' staggered towards the bed. He felt his life fluid ebbing out of him. Still he was animated by that great burning rage which had made him kill so many times before. The old man *had* to die! Nothing else mattered. Slowly he started to bring those huge hams of his down, as the General sat there as if mesmerized, his skinny old limbs tensed for what had to come.

The 'Beast' mouthed obscenities, a red haze threatening to envelop him. His blood fell to the floor and on to the white fur rug in great red gobs. He staggered and seemed about to fall, but he recovered and continued advancing while the General watched him, the full horror of what was going to happen slowly revealing itself on his raddled face. 'No, no!' he cried suddenly as the 'Beast' reached out his hands, the hairy fingers searching for the GOC's skinny neck. *'NO, PLEASE!'*

Ginger burst through the door. He took in the scene immediately. 'None o' that, there 'ere!' he yelled and flung himself at the 'Beast', his cosh raised. The 'Beast' brushed him aside with one swipe of his left arm which sent Ginger flying helplessly against the wardrobe. The glass splintered and the boxes on top of it showered down on

Ginger, who lay there racked with pain.

Billy Bennett, panting, his face red and lathered with sweat, followed. He raised his revolver. Behind him CPO Ferguson yelled urgently, 'Put yon gun down, ye bluidy fool ... ye might hit the General. Grab hold o' him!'

Billy, as big and as broad as the 'Beast', clubbed the revolver by the muzzle and rushed into the fight. The 'Beast' didn't seem to even notice the blow that Billy slammed into his shoulder. He merely shook his head like a bull importuned in summer by a swarm of cheeky flies. 'Christ,' Billy cursed, 'the man's like a ruddy ox!' He smashed his revolver down on the 'Beast's' shaven skull.

The 'Beast' roared with sudden rage. He forgot the General for a moment and lashed out with a fist like a small steam shovel. Billy went flying, blood spurting out in thick rich snorts from his shattered nose. CPO Ferguson reacted with surprising speed for such an old man. He yelled at the General. 'Fall on the floor, sir. *NO – QUICK!*'

The General dropped instantly and in that same moment, CPO Ferguson fired. The impact of the slug at such short range flung the 'Beast' off his feet, as the bullet struck him directly in his face. The years of plastic surgery disintegrated in a flash. The nose flew off as did the artificial jaw. Abruptly a huge hole appeared in the centre of his face, filled with gore and broken bones which glistened like polished ivory against that scarlet background.

Fighting his fate to the very last, the 'Beast' tried to struggle to his feet while the Englishmen watched in horrified fascination. He managed to raise himself on one knee, hectic sucking noises coming from the hole which sank in and out every time he breathed. Then he gave a soft keening moan and pitched forward, head first, dead before he touched the floor.

For what seemed an age all of them froze, like bad actors at the end of an even worse melodrama, each man trapped by his own horror and sense of shock at this terrible sight. Then Smith spoke slowly in a voice that he hardly recognized as his own. He said, 'Ferguson, help the General to his feet.' Then to the General. 'Perhaps you should cover yourself – or dress – before our authorities arrive to investigate.'

'Thank you ... thank you very much,' the GOC replied in a very shaky voice. 'I will do as you wish.' With hands that trembled badly, he reached for his silk khaki shirt and, with some difficulty because he was shaking so much, pulled it over his head.

While he did so, Smith went over to the inert body. With the toe of his shoe, for he didn't trust himself to touch the dead killer, he turned him over so that that terrible face was hidden from view, feeling the hot, choking bile rise up in his throat as he did so.

'Thank God you did that, Smithie,' Dickie Bird said with feeling. 'Couldn't have stood that face much longer – or what's left of it.' He sighed. 'Well, it's all over now I suppose.' He looked at Smith and then at the General, busy climbing into his breeches. Smith nodded and Dickie said formally, 'I think we ought to go now, sir.'

The GOC paused, one skinny white leg halfway into the breeches. He thought of the girl still in the bathroom and said, 'Yes, I think I'll be all right now. Thank you again, gentlemen.'

The two officers clicked to attention and a still groggy Ginger and Billy tried to do the same, after a threatening look had been shot in their direction by CPO Ferguson, who said, 'Sir, I'll ask the West Yorks to send up some of yon squaddies to clear up,' he indicated the shattered body on the floor, and left the sentence unfinished.

'Yes, I'd appreciate that, Petty Officer,' the General said. 'It is rather messy.'

NINE

She listened to the sound of their boots vanishing down into the hall, purse, with the pistol inside it, clutched in her hands tightly. What was she to do? She guessed that the killer had failed because she had just heard the General's voice. He was still alive.

She tried to calm herself and think clearly. The other English had seen her come in. But did they know she was still there? She was sure that the General wouldn't have mentioned her presence. That would have been too embarrassing for him. But if she did what she now knew she had to do, how would she get away? There was a cordon of troops and police around the villa. She wouldn't be able to sneak through them without being apprehended.

Suddenly she remembered the Rolls Royce. They wouldn't stop the General's car. They'd assume that she had stayed after all and the chauffeur would be taking her home now, nice and discreetly.

She bit her bottom lip as she tried to work out the problem. The chauffeur was dead, she was sure of that. The killer had been ordered to assassinate him, too, so that there would be no witness to her involvement in the assassination. Then her face lit up. Of course, that would be it.

She'd put on the dead chauffeur's cap and greatcoat. In the dim light of this rain-swept night she'd pass as a man. Her own coat would be draped in the back of the Rolls, as if she were slumped in sleep there. That would be her escape route. She frowned again. But could she commit the murder, even if it was for the holy cause of the New Fatherland – and the future prosperity of the von Duckwitz family?

Suddenly she realized that her role in the assassination of the General had been changed completely. As von Horn had planned it, she had been merely a tool, an auxiliary to the murderer. She would have dealt with the assassin and then would have vanished quietly into the obscurity of Switzerland for months, perhaps even years, while the great events in Germany took their course. She would not even have been a footnote in the history of the revolution to come. Now she had the opportunity to be a central character, a worthy successor to three hundred years of von Duckwitzs who had served first Prussia, then Imperial Germany with fame and honours heaped upon them.

She looked at her own image in the mirror above the bath. Underneath all that beauty she saw the strong jaw and determined set of the face possessed by generations of her ancestors. She was one of them – and proud to be so.

Now there was no going back, she told herself. She was alone in the house with the General. He would be easy meat for her.

There was a gentle knock on the door of the bathroom. 'Darling,' the General enquired, 'are you all right?'

Swiftly she opened her purse and took out the little pearl-handled revolver. 'Yes,' she answered in that little girl's voice that he liked. 'Has something happened?'

'Yes, I'm afraid there has been a little unpleasantness. Deuced rotten really. Spoiled our Saturday evening, what. But perhaps we can make up for it during the week.'

'Of course, darling. You shall have some really special treatment next time.' Softly, very softly so that he wouldn't hear, she slipped off the safety catch and gripped the pistol more tightly.

'Oh, I say,' he chortled, the shock of what had just happened vanished now. 'That's dashed sporting of you, m'dear.' He swallowed hard. 'Something *really* special?' he echoed.

'Yes,' she said through gritted tecth, reaching for the knob with her free hand. 'You won't be springing out of bed after that so quickly.'

'Gosh!' he breathed. 'I can hardly wait. Pity that I'll have to get you out now. But the police will be coming soon to clear up the mess and undoubtedly there'll be questions and all that stuff. It's much better that you're out of the house by then. We don't want any scandal, do we? Hopkins will take you home nice and discreetly.'

She didn't answer. She was concentrating totally on her task. Her knuckles whitened as she gripped the little pistol even tighter. As soon as the door was opened, she'd fire. Immediately. There had to be no time to think – and hesitate. She took her own hand off the knob, changing her plan a little so that she had both hands available.

'Why don't you come in, General. I'm nearly dressed. But if you'd like to give me a good-bye kiss...'

'My word,' the General exclaimed in delight. 'I don't suppose that you've got your dress off and that you're clad in your – er – frillies?'

'I'm still in my underwear, General, if you would like a little peep before I finally get dressed.'

'I'm coming in then,' he quavered, hardly able to suppress his excitement, everything else forgotten. *'Now!'*

The door handle started to turn. She waited there, pistol raised, hand holding it as steady as a rock.

McIntyre took it all in in a flash. The half open door; the General with the look of a lecherous old goat on his raddled face; the outline of the girl in the bathroom mirror – and the gun she had levelled at the door.

'*Duck,* sir!' he roared at the General, reacting instinctively. He dare not use his revolver in case he hit the General. Instead, he used the only weapon at hand – his cap. With a savage jerk, he threw it at the woman. The cap, with its stiffened brim, hissed across the room like a discus... The girl yelped with pain as the brim, with the sharp-edged badge, caught her full in the face. She staggered back, banged into the edge of the bath, overbalanced and fell backwards into it.

On his knees at the door, the General caught, what would be his last glimpse, of those deliciously spread legs, with the patch of sheer black silk in between, barely hiding that source of all delight. Then McIntyre was through the door in a mad rush. He picked up the girl by the front of her dress. It ripped open and her breasts spilled out. The gun tumbled from her hand. Next moment he drew back his fist and slammed it hard into her pretty mouth. She went out like a light.

'I say, you can't do that,' the General breathed, shocked. 'After all she's a lady.'

‘She’s no lady – and I’ve done it,’ McIntyre gasped.

Then he felt all his energy drain out of him, as if someone had opened a tap. The case was closed. He had done it. He leaned against the wall, as the General quavered into the phone down to the guardhouse below, from which came the sound of heavy boots running, ‘I say, would you send someone up? There’s been a bit of an accident…’

TEN

The sky hung grey and leaden above Munich. It was bitterly cold and snow was forecast. But despite the cold, the streets of the Bavarian capital were packed with people: civilians, soldiers, police and Party members in their brown uniforms. Tension was in the air. For all of them knew, whatever side they were on, that on this day the issue would be settled one way or another.

In the unheated hotel room in the *Odeonplatz,* the four men, clad in their overcoats, waited, peering through the tall french windows for the first sign of the marchers. Far off they could hear the muted brass of a military band and down below the crowd was already craning their necks in anticipation.

C broke the heavy silence. He said drily, 'It won't be long now, Herr von Stein, I don't suppose. Will your police fire now?'

Herr von Stein, bearded, old, sunk into the fur collar of his coat, said a little wearily, 'Hope so, *Herr Admiral.* I fervently hope so. We have had too many of these–' he clicked his gloved fingers impatiently at not being able to find the word in English.

'Uprisings, sir,' Smith volunteered the word.

'Yes, thank you. Uprisings. Yes, we have had too many of them since the war. Let us pray that this will be the last one and then we shall have peace.'

Down below a scuffle had broken out in the waiting crowd. '*Jude*,' half a dozen men in the Party's brown uniform were crying angrily, punching a small man, while a woman, screaming violently, was trying to pull them off him.

'A Jew,' the man from Berlin explained in that same weary manner he had displayed ever since they had met him in Berlin two days before. 'These Nazis, as we call the National Socialists, hate the Jews – and us, too.' He gave the three Englishmen a tired smile.

The capture of Kati von Duckwitz and her confession had done the trick. The British ambassador had made an immediate protest to the German government in Berlin. C had supplied him with the fullest documentation: how the attempted assassination of the General Officer Commanding the British Army of the Rhine was to be the signal for a right-wing revolt in Munich under the leadership of Adolf Hitler, which would, in the end, topple the government in Berlin. The socialist government had decided to act. But as von Stein had said at their first meeting in his *Reichstag* office, 'Can we trust the army – the police?'

'How do you mean, sir?' C had asked sharply.

'The officers of both the army and the police are mostly right-wing. Will they fire on their own kind, even to defend the Constitution?' And again he had shrugged in that weary manner of his, as if the whole world was simply too much for him to bear.

Now positioned in this cold, upper-storey hotel room, with a thin cordon of police blocking the street further up the road and another line down at the bottom, they waited to see what would happen. Would the 'Austrian rabble-rouser', as von Stein had called him, both contempt and fear in his voice, succeed after all?

The sound of the march music came closer and closer. Down at the cordons, the green-uniformed police started to shuffle their feet awkwardly and the watchers could see the looks of doubt and confusion on their faces, as they awaited the first sign from the marchers.

'There they are!' Dickie cried.

Eight abreast, packing the narrow street from side to side, the brown-clad marchers came surging up the Residenzstrasse, singing and cheering, periodically throwing up their arms in the new Nazi greeting and shouting 'Heil Hitler' to well-wishers hanging out of the windows on both sides of the street.

Von Stein lifted the glasses he had brought with them and focused them on the front rankers of the marchers, arms linked together as they bellowed, *'O Deutschland hoch in Ehren.'**

'Verdammt!' he exclaimed, 'they've got General Ludendorff marching with them. God, what will the police do now.'

All of them knew who Ludendorff was. He had been virtually the military dictator of Imperial Germany for the last years of the war. If he had thrown in his lot with the Nazis, they had to be taken seriously. Now Smith could see where von Horn had got his backing from: Ludendorff, the most senior and important ex-Imperial Army officer.

'That's Captain Goering,' von Stein continued, 'and there's that chap with the moustache, that's the Austrian – Hitler.'

Both Smith and Dickie Bird raised their glasses. A dark, flushed, angry face came sliding into the gleaming circle of calibrated glass. They saw the ugly toothbrush moustache and the lock of lank black hair hanging down over the Austrian's brow. 'Not exactly the face to set the world on

**O Germany high in honour.*

fire,' Dickie Bird commented airily.

'I don't know,' Smith said thoughtfully and slowly, lowering his glasses. 'There's something about that man's face – I can't exactly put my finger on it – something evil, infinitely evil, perhaps.'

At the first police cordon, at the entrance to the Odeonplatz, the harassed policemen were ordering the marchers to stop. But they had no success. The cheering, booing crowd swept them to one side and surged onwards, yelling *'Heil Hitler ... Heil Hitler'* with fanatical fervour.

Von Stein lowered his glasses. *'Himmelherrje,* they didn't even attempt to unsling their rifles and fire a few warning shots over the mob's head. We're lost ... we're lost!' He started to wring his skinny hands and looking at him, C told himself he knew why the Berlin Government was a failure. It was made up of too many weaklings like von Stein. He cleared his throat angrily.

Now the marching mob was approaching the last police cordon. Behind it lay the great *Felderrnhalle,* where it was expected that Hitler would declare the state of Bavaria was now in National Socialist hands, the first step in his take-over of the whole of Germany. Then the Republic would be finished.

All four of the watchers concentrated their attention on the pale-faced young police officer who had stepped out into the middle of the street. Alone, he faced the advancing mob. In a loud voice, he called, 'The march is illegal! In the name of the Free State of Bavaria I order you to disperse!'

The mob faltered, such was the look of grim determination on the young officer's pale, aristocratic face. Hitler shouted something and slashed his calf angrily with the dog whip he was carrying. The mob surged forward again.

The police officer turned. 'Second company, double time, *march!*'

Hurriedly, the green-uniformed policemen, carrying their rifles at the slope, doubled forward.

Now the leaders of the mob were almost up to the lone officer. He brought his own rifle down to his hip, standing there ready for anything, it seemed.

Someone in the mob lunged at him with a bayonet. He parried the thrust easily. Nazis started firing their pistols. At first in the air. But as the police officer brought one of their number down to his knees with a blow from his rifle butt, they started to fire at the police company. A shot howled off the wall next to the lone officer, showering him with brick splinters. Another whizzed over his head. Behind him, the leading police sergeant clutched his chest. A sudden stain coloured his tunic a bright scarlet. Wordlessly, without even a moan, he fell to the cobbles.

The death of their sergeant acted like a signal to the harassed policemen. They fired a salvo into the mob. Nazis went down everywhere, screaming, shrieking, clutching their wounded limbs. Frantically the mob started to scramble for safety.

Suddenly, Smith was willing the Austrian Hitler to be hit and killed. Somehow he knew, with the one hundred per cent certainty of a vision, that that world would be a safer and better place if Hitler died *now.*

That wasn't to be. A small man leapt in front of the Party leader. Smith could see the bullets thwacking into the unknown protector's body. He went down, dragging Hitler with him, his body still acting as a shield for the prostrate leader.

Now the dead and dying lay everywhere on the blood-stained cobbles, with a man who had been hit in both legs trying to crawl away, as the back of the mob hesitated, wavered, wondered if they were hearing small arms fire or the explosions of fireworks which were going to be used to celebrate their take-over of power in Munich.

Smith and the rest watched, fascinated, as the police rifles still at their hips, started to move forward to where the dead and wounded lay. 'Take him!' von Stein exclaimed suddenly with angry fervour, 'take that Austrian swine into custody!'

But already the Austrian had struggled to his feet, cradling one arm in his other hand, as if he had hurt the limb. A giant rushed to his assistance. The man, who towered a head higher than Hitler, moved away from the police more quickly, dragging the injured leader with him. Moments later they had disappeared round a corner, the mob vanishing with them, leaving the narrow street to the police and the dead sprawled out in the extravagant angles and poses of those done violently to death.

In the hotel room, after the noise and excitement of the last few minutes, there was a sudden brooding silence, as if each man was wrapped up in a cocoon of his own thoughts.

'Well,' C said finally, taking von Stein's arm as if they were the oldest of friends, 'I think we all deserve a strong drink.'

'*Einverstanden,*' von Stein agreed, suddenly smiling, as if a great weight had been taken off his mind. 'Berlin has had a triumph this day.'

'I think you're right,' C said. 'It looks as if you Germans have seen the back of that Austrian chap – what's his name?'

'Hitler.'

'That's right, Hitler. Good riddance to bad rubbish.' Chatting happily together, as if they had both been members of C's club, White's, for ages, they went out and disappeared down the stairs to the bar below.

Dickie looked at Smith. 'A penny for them, old bean?'

'I was just thinking.'

'What?'

'Hard for me to put it into words, Dickie. Come on, let's sting old C for a free drink. It's not that often that our dear leader pushes out the boat.'

They followed the two older men down to the bar. Outside the police company was marching away, rifles slung, job done, leaving the street to the medics and their assistants. 'Bloodhounds!' the mob shrieked, shaking their fists at the police and spitting on them. *Pfui,* Jew lovers ... betrayers of the Fatherland ... Heil Hitler!'

Opposite, a fat man, who wore the medal of the *Pour la Merite* around his neck and had been wounded in the firing, was asking to be admitted to a big house so that he could escape arrest. 'But this is the house of Jews,' the owner was protesting. 'No matter,' the wounded man was gasping frantically, 'I'm the war hero, Captain Goering of the Richthofen Squadron. You must have heard of me? I can't stand the shame of being arrested by the police. Please let me in ... *please.*'

'You asked me a minute ago, Dickie – a

penny for my thoughts,' Smith said as he turned into the bar, 'Well, I'll tell you. Frankly, I don't think we've seen the end of Mr Hitler – by a long chalk. Look at all that hate and feeling out there. It won't just go away – like that. No, Dickie,' Smith added, his handsome young face set and stern. 'Mr Hitler'll be back sooner or later, like a bad penny, I'll be bound.'

Smith's words didn't seem to worry Dickie Bird. He said happily enough, 'Then, old bean, we'll have to see him off again, won't we. Now let's see about getting that free drink out of old C…'

ENVOI

'Splice the Mainbrace!'

The Prime Minister wallowed in his bath. His false teeth gaped obscenely from a glass at the side of the bath. In one soap-covered hand he held a glass of whisky and soda. In the other, there was a fat, expensive double Corona cigar. He looked like a pink, hairless, glistening Buddha.

Happily, he listened to the wireless blaring away in his bedroom next door. The BBC announcer was giving the details of the latest Allied victories in Germany. They were coming in fast and furiously. On every front the Allies were overwhelmingly, totally victorious. Montgomery's armies had reached the German Baltic coast. Patton had swept right through Germany and was now marching towards Prague in Czechoslovakia. The Russians had completely surrounded Berlin and it was confidently expected that the German capital would fall within days, perhaps even hours.

'John, my dear boy,' the Prime Minister lisped to his secretary, young John Colville, sitting at the side of the big bath, 'the Hun is absolutely, totally whipped – *at last!*'

John Colville, clad in the uniform of a pilot in the RAF, looked down at the Prime Minister and told himself that Winston

Churchill had never looked happier. After six years as the 'King's First Minister', as he always called himself, the PM had brought the nation to victory.

Suddenly, the wireless went dead for a moment. When the announcer came on the air again and spoke, his typical BBC well-modulated tones could not quite conceal the excitement in his voice. 'We have just heard from Berlin, the following message read out by the German naval commander Admiral Doenitz.' He cleared his throat. 'German men and woman, soldiers of the German *Wehrmacht!* Our Fuhrer, Adolf Hitler, has fallen. The German people bow in deepest mourning and veneration. He recognized beforehand the terrible danger of Bolshevism and devoted his life to fighting it. At the end of this, his battle, and of his unswerving path in life, he stands, in death, as a hero in the capital of the Reich... That is the end of the German message.'

Churchill looked up at Colville, his eyes glowing with joy and pride. 'We've done it, John! The beast is dead at last. Forget that gruff about his heroic death etc. That's been carefully invented with an eye to the future Hitler myth and legend. In all probability, he blew his own brains out.' He took a deep drink of his whisky and soda.

'John,' Churchill continued, after draining the last drop of his drink, 'you know nothing about this. Long ago, Hitler tried to have me killed. Obviously he didn't succeed. But now *I've* seen him off. Now I want you to signal the Admiralty and have them contact Common Smith VC.'

Colville looked up from his pad in bewilderment. 'Common Smith VC?'

'Long before your time, my boy. Just write what I say.' He waved his cigar in the air as if it were a pen.

'Yes PM.'

'To Common Smith VC, then. Tuesday May 1st, 1945... It has taken 22 years since that first encounter on the Rhine. At last he has met his just retribution. Hitler is dead!' the PM looked up at Colville, 'Sign it WSC. Oh yes, and add this postscript – splice the mainbrace.'

Colville looked up from his pad. 'Highly irregular, sir,' he said. 'Their Lordships won't like that.'

'Damn their Lordships,' Churchill growled. He poked the big cigar in the direction of his own hairless white chest, 'I'm in charge of the Royal Navy, Splice the mainbrace, it is...'

Four hours later, Captain de Vere Smith, VCDO, DSC sat back in his leather armchair in the flotilla captain's cabin and read the signal from their Lordships once again. Outside, the convoy his flotilla was escorting from Boston to Greenock, wallowed in the dark green sea, which sparkled in the May sunshine. But at that moment the hard-faced flotilla captain was thinking of the muddy brown water of the Rhine of that fateful year so long ago.

They were all dead now, save Dickie Bird, who was somewhere in the Med. Poor Chiefie Ferguson had gone down with the *Glorious* in '40. Ginger Kerrigan had not been one of the three survivors of the *Hood* when the Bismarck had sunk her a year later. Billy Bennett, still the barrel of lard he had been in the '20's, had lasted till '42 when the Japs had sunk the *Prince of Wales*, that brand-new battleship of which he had been so proud. One by one the old crew of the *Swordfish* had been killed by that monster whom he had seen lying hurt in that Munich street...

Tears welled up in his eyes at the thought and he hoped they would somehow know, wherever they were, in heaven or hell, that they had been finally avenged. He wiped the tears from his eyes. It wouldn't do for a flotilla chief to be seen weeping, he told himself. He rang the bell on his desk. The chief steward came in immediately and stood to attention. 'Chiefie,' Smith barked in a voice thickened by years of pink gins and shouting orders in force twelve gales, 'tell the bosun to splice the mainbrace.'

'Splice the mainbrace, sir!' the steward

said in astonishment. 'Now?'

'Yes now,' Smith answered, his face breaking into a wintry smile. 'Don't you know? We've got something to celebrate. *HITLER IS DEAD!*'

AUTHOR'S NOTE

When German Kati von Duckwitz died last year aged 90, her funeral in Bayreuth was attended by over 300 Neo-Nazis. It is doubtful if many of the shaven-haired louts, who gave the forbidden Hitler salute at her graveside, watched by tense, expectant police in their leather riot gear, really knew who she was. All they probably knew is that in the early days of the Nazi Party she had tried to help Hitler to power, and that after she had returned from English imprisonment, Hitler had personally awarded her the 'Order of the Blood'.*

But in the fragments and papers that Captain de Vere Smith, VC, had left behind on his death three years previously, Kati von Duckwitz is mentioned very frequently. 'Scheming, pretty little minx', is one of his descriptions of Fraulein von Duckwitz. 'A would-be murderess who didn't hesitate to use her undoubted sexual charms to achieve her purpose', is another. All pretty strong

*Awarded to those who had been imprisoned or shed their blood before the Party had come to power in 1933.

stuff for 'Common Smith VC', as he was universally known in England in the '20's. For Smith was a typical upper-class Englishman of his time. He was not given easily to displaying his emotions or feelings about other people, especially when those other people were women, or 'the fair sex', as he was wont to call them.

Though he had 'adventured' (as he put it) all over Europe, illegally running guns to the new Poland on behalf of the British Secret Service, helping to prevent the massacre of the Greeks in Turkey during the Turco-Greek War, he had never been closer to failing a mission as when he had come up against the beautiful and fanatical Fraulein von Duckwitz. Right to the bitter end, she had almost fooled him and his shipmates of the *Swordfish*. It was only in the nick of time that Common Smith VC, was able to foil the plot, which would have helped Hitler to power in *1923* and not ten years later in *1933*.

That ten-year difference saved Britain, and Europe, from perpetual Nazi domination which would have probably lasted to this very day. *Sixteen* years of Nazi power in Germany instead of *six* would have given the Third Reich an absolutely unstoppable war machine in 1939 at the outbreak of World War Two. *Britain – and Europe – in the 1990s have a lot to thank Common Smith VC for.*

C.W.

The publishers hope that this book has given you enjoyable reading. Large Print Books are especially designed to be as easy to see and hold as possible. If you wish a complete list of our books please ask at your local library or write directly to:

This Large Print Book, for people
who cannot read normal print,
is published under the auspices of

THE ULVERSCROFT FOUNDATION

... we hope you have enjoyed this book.
Please think for a moment about those
who have worse eyesight than you ...
and are unable to even read or enjoy
Large Print without great difficulty.

You can help them by sending a
donation, large or small, to:

**The Ulverscroft Foundation,
1, The Green, Bradgate Road,
Anstey, Leicestershire, LE7 7FU,
England.**
or request a copy of our brochure for
more details.

The Foundation will use all donations
to assist those people who are visually
impaired and need special attention
with medical research, diagnosis
and treatment.

Thank you very much for your help.

B1	09/17
FL [illegible]	03/20 [illegible]
LB	3/21
SF	03/25